Praise for Mary Calmes and her novel

I0659425

Change *of* Heart

As a young gay man—and a werepanther—all Jin Rayne yearns for is a normal life. Having fled his past, he wants nothing more than to start over, but Jin's old life doesn't want to let him go. When his travels bring him to a new city, he crosses paths with the leader of the local were-tribe. Logan Church is a shock and an enigma, and Jin fears that Logan is both the mate he fears and the love of his life. Jin doesn't want to go back to the old ways, and mating would irrevocably tie him to them.

But Jin is the mate Logan needs at his side to help him lead his tribe, and he won't give Jin up so easily. It will take time and trust for Jin to discover the joy in belonging to Logan and how to love without restraint.

This engrossing story will keep the reader's attention till the very last page.

—Rainbow Reviews

The story draws you in from the first scene and never releases its hold until the final sentence.

—Literary Nymphs Reviews

The GUARDIAN

Mary Calmes

Dreamspinner Press

Published by
Dreamspinner Press
4760 Preston Road
Suite 244-149
Frisco, TX 75034
http://www.dreamspinnerpress.com/

Cover Art by Anne Cain   annecain.art@gmail.com
Cover Design by Mara McKennen

ISBN: 978-1-61581-380-3

Printed in the United States of America
First Edition
February, 2010

eBook edition available
eBook ISBN: 978-1-61581-381-0

This one is for my husband,
who thinks he doesn't help,

for Elizabeth and Lynn
at Dreamspinner,
who do,

and for my family and friends,
for all theirs.

Chapter One

IT WAS hard to explain what it was that woke him. Even trying later to put the experience into words, Jude found it impossible. One minute he was lost in a dream, the very next he was wide awake, panting, sitting up in bed in a cold sweat. *What in the world?* He felt like he was drowning and squeezed in a vise all at the same time. When he tried to go back to sleep that proved futile. The overwhelming feeling of dread would not budge; he needed to get up or something horrible would happen. So even though it made no sense, he rolled out of bed and went to the bathroom. Looking into his own dark brown eyes in the mirror, he realized that maybe it was just his own life that had him awake at three in the morning. Lately it seemed like a pit had opened up and he couldn't pull free. Nothing was going right, and with no end in sight, it made sense that panic would leap from his subconscious, where he kept it pinned down all day, and grab hold of him while he was sleeping. But even as he told himself that the fear was logical, he still couldn't shake it. Maybe if he took a walk he'd feel better; his one-bedroom apartment felt small suddenly and claustrophobic. He had to get out.

After pulling on jeans, a heavy wool sweater, and hiking boots, twenty-six-year-old Jude Shea made his way from his brownstone toward the park. It was slow going, colder than he thought it would be, but being outside worked to clear his head. He felt calmer, steadier, grounded… until he heard the growling. Turning the corner he realized that he had made a left instead of a right. He had meant to take the path over the footbridge but had ended up going under it instead and now found himself at the mouth of a small tunnel. From where he was he could see the moon-washed path on the other side, could see the barren trees and even the wrought-iron fence, but between him and that was the total darkness of the creepy, smelly tunnel. And something close by was growling.

It took only a second to decide to reverse his course and go back, but in that heartbeat of time, he felt something resonate inside him. It was the pulse again, the same throb, a pressure that pushed against him like a sonic wave, like something or someone was calling to him. Jude had never felt anything like it and found it hard to process, to categorize. There was no pain, just the feeling of falling, like the first drop on a rollercoaster. He shivered hard, deciding quickly that nothing would keep him from moving forward. The pull was too strong to ignore. He had to find whatever it was he was outside in the cold looking for, because maybe if he found it, the hollow feeling in the pit of his stomach would go away. He could only hope.

As Jude strode into the dark tunnel, he felt stupid for even hesitating. The growling had obviously been just the howl of the wind. He was not a woman who had to worry about being attacked, and at five-eleven and covered in lean muscle, there were not a lot of men who could hurt him without a weapon of some kind. Really, the only thing he had to worry about at all was finding a job. Having been looking for one for the last two weeks, he was exhausted. He had no business being out of bed at three in the morning looking for what... something that had drawn him with its siren call? It was crazy, and yet he plowed on through the pitch black of the tunnel to the other side.

When he emerged, the second he came around the corner, he saw them. There were four dogs in all, three on their feet and one on the ground. The three that were hovering were taking turns biting and clawing at the prone figure. The snarling was loud, the attack was vicious, and the dog that could no longer fight back would be dead soon. A feeling of relief washed over him, and he knew, beyond anything remotely logical, that he was there to save the dog. He yelled, and there was instant silence but for the moan of the wind. It had rained earlier, and between the wet chill in the air, the black shapes outlined against a dark charcoal sky, and the way the leaves blew across the path, there was an eerie feel to the night. When the dogs turned on him and charged, heads lowered, he felt as though he were facing some primordial foe instead of feral dogs in the park. Even for someone as rational as Jude, there was a second of horror before he heard the laughter.

Turning, he saw the group of people emerge from the tunnel. Four men, three women—and the first guy on the end reached under his jacket as he called out "Hey, man, you all right?"

The guy had a gun, and normally a man with a gun outside of law enforcement would be a concern, but right then the only thing Jude could be was thankful. He took a breath so his heart could start again.

"What the fuck's goin' on?" another of the men asked.

Turning back to face the dogs, Jude realized instantly that they were gone. "Where did they go?"

"That way," one of the guys said as the group reached him, pointing into the trees to the left. "Man, you are all kinds of crazy."

Jude didn't waste another second of time. Charging up the slight incline, he fell to his knees beside the injured animal. It was enormous, not as big as the others—their size had been freakish—but still the biggest dog Jude had ever seen.

"Oh shit," someone said behind him.

The dog lifted its head just barely and looked at its savior before the snarl tore from his throat. The sound made everyone except Jude shudder.

"Ohmygod, don't touch him!" a woman exclaimed.

"Get back! He'll rip your arm off!" a man warned.

Jude was too close to the wounded animal. If the dog wanted to, it could tear out his throat or maul the hand reaching toward him. There could be no protection from an attack in the slight distance between them.

Nothing mattered to Jude but the fact that the dog was hurt and needed him. Every other concern paled in comparison. The second he felt the wet heavy breath on his skin, Jude knew it would be all right. He smoothed his hand over the dog's nose, and its tongue darted out to lick his fingers. Scooting forward, cradling the dog's head in his hands, Jude gently, tenderly, put the heavy skull down on his bent knees. The dog's whimper was almost painful to hear as it pushed forward, trying to get its body closer to the man. Jude knew the animal had to be freezing, it was shaking with pain and fatigue, but its innate need for human contact still had overcome its instinct for self-preservation. The dog wanted to be in the man's lap.

"It's okay, baby, I got you," Jude promised the dog as its eyes started to droop closed.

There was a chorus of *oh* from the women, assorted groans, and finally the command from the first guy to *help the fuckin' guy with his goddamn dog*. Jude looked up at the man with a leather trench coat over his black Versace suit and thanked him.

"You are one lucky sonofabitch." The man smiled down at Jude, the diamond in his front tooth catching the light. "What the hell were you thinkin', walkin' up on a wounded animal?"

"He needed me," Jude said helplessly.

"Yeah, well, I suggest maybe you use your brain next time."

There was always a first time.

WHO woke up in the middle of the night and ended up saving a dog? The story was crazy, but even more amazing was the fact that no one cared. The nice lady at the intake window at the county animal shelter, the vet tech who took the dog from him, as well as the vet herself, none of them were interested in what had led him to the dog, only with the fact that he had saved it. He was a hero, plain and simple, and they all took turns telling him that.

Hours later, as he sat in the waiting area filling out forms, he found himself stuck on *Name of Animal* and couldn't get any further. There was no way he could be responsible for a dog when his entire life was up in the air. How could he promise to feed and shelter another life when he didn't even have a job? Sitting there, staring down at the linoleum floor, it was hard not to sink into self-pity.

A month ago, the small, financially sound public relations firm where Jude had worked for the past three years had been acquired by Sheridan Grant, a behemoth in the industry with offices all across country. The impact was that there had been many layoffs and only very few jobs had been spared. Jude had been one of the lucky ones—his reputation and client list kept the wolves from his door—but job security ended up being the least of his problems. A new managing director had been chosen for their office and Colton Bale showed up fresh from San Francisco with big ideas for change. Jude had no idea at the time what that meant for him personally.

"Excuse me, uh, Mr. Shea?"

Yanked from his reverie, Jude looked up into the face of the vet tech. She was a very pretty girl with a cute ponytail, and her nametag identified her as Amy. He found her adorable but completely missed his effect on her.

With his big dark brown eyes, impossibly long lashes, chiseled features, and flawless skin, the man was as close to perfection as she would ever see. She swallowed her gum.

"Um, can you come with me?"

"Sure," he replied, standing. "But don't call me 'sir,' call me Jude."

"Jude," she repeated, her eyes looking him over from head to toe. *Yummy.* The man was definitely edible with his curly brown hair that fell just past his shoulders, full, kissable lips, and lean frame. The jeans were tight and hugged long legs, and when she let him walk in front of her for a moment, she saw a firm, round ass. He was pretty, and she liked her men that way.

Jude checked over his shoulder, not sure which way to go once they hit the hall and confused as to why he was leading when he had no idea where he was going. Amy pointed to his right and then did a quick step and was back in front of him. Walking into a room three doors down, Jude was again faced with Dr. Rosalie Powers, the on-site veterinarian. He decided that she was the kind of woman that men—straight men—would watch walk by on the street: striking, with her waves of chestnut hair and blue eyes. Since he was gay, he noted her allure, but it was lost on him.

"Mr. Shea, I—" the vet started.

"Jude," he cut her off, yawning. "It's too late, or early, I guess, for Mr. Shea."

Dr. Powers's smile was warm. "Well, Jude, let's talk about your dog."

His dog?

He was told that his pet—the horse masquerading as a dog—was most likely a Newfoundland/husky or malamute mix. He had been viciously cut up and bitten, and it also looked like he had been struck hard by something. Dr. Powers thought perhaps he had been hit by a car, and then some other dogs had seen him, judged him incapacitated, and attacked him. Whatever the situation, he was lucky to be alive, and he was also a marvel of healing. The X-rays had yielded no broken bones, but his ribs were badly bruised. That he was already able to stand was amazing. He had drunk some water but was refusing to eat. She wanted to keep him overnight, but the problem was she didn't think she could.

"How'dya mean?" Jude asked.

It was like Dr. Powers was almost embarrassed. "I don't think even the big kennel will hold him. He's just too big. I need to keep him in the wolf enclosure at the zoo or something."

Wolf enclosure? How big was the dog really?

"So maybe you should just take him home, and I'll give you the name of a vet, and Monday morning you can take him in just to have him looked at."

Jude was surprised. "Are you serious?"

To show him that she was in no way kidding, the vet tech, Amy, cheerfully presented Jude with a bill for three hundred and twenty-two dollars and seventy-four cents. They were *so* not kidding.

"Wait!" He put up his hands. "I can't have a dog. I have a one-bedroom apartment that's like seven hundred square feet."

"Lucky it's a one-bedroom." Amy smiled at him.

"Yes," Dr. Powers agreed, "because that guy's a monster."

"Guy?"

Dr. Powers grinned at him, nodding. "Congratulations, Mr. Shea. It's a boy."

"Wait," he told her. "I seriously *can't* have a dog."

"Not a lot of people could accommodate a dog that big."

"That's not what I mean."

"No pets allowed in your building?" Dr. Powers asked.

"No, but—"

"You allergic?"

"No, I just—"

Dr. Powers chuckled deeply. "Jude, I suggest you put an ad in the paper and try to find his owner. He's in much too good shape to be a stray, and let's face it, as big as he is, somebody's missing him. A dog like that doesn't just fall from the sky."

Jude sighed deeply as an overwhelming sense of resignation came over him.

"Someone will come claim him, Jude, I promise you."

But his luck didn't work like that.

"Think about it this way. You'll never have to worry about being robbed again. Who in their right mind would even try?" Dr. Powers reasoned.

He shot her a look.

Her laughter bubbled up out of her; the smile was huge. "I mean really, who in their right mind would rob a man who has a wolf?"

"He's not a wolf," he mumbled.

"No, he's probably a cross between a Newfoundland or a Great Pyrenees and something else. Except for the shape of his ears and his muzzle, he looks like one of those to me. But his nose and the shape of his head suggest a sled dog. It might even seriously be wolf in there; I have no way of knowing. But he's a huge dog. He weighs just over a hundred and twenty pounds, and it's all muscle. There's not an ounce of fat on him."

He groaned.

"I have no space for a dog that big at this facility," Dr. Powers said apologetically.

"I don't either," Jude assured her.

"Then I suggest you find his owner."

"What if he tries to bite me?"

"If he tries to bite you, I wouldn't worry about it." Dr. Powers sighed deeply.

"Why not?"

"Because Mr. Shea, if he goes after you, you're going to die."

Jude wondered vaguely if she was allowed to say those kinds of things to him. Wasn't she supposed to be encouraging?

When Dr. Powers smacked him on the shoulder, he got that she understood that she could. Most people were quickly at ease with Jude, and the nice lady vet was proving to be no exception. Jude's father always told him it was a gift, the warmth he radiated that drew people like bees to honey. Jude had never been fully convinced.

The dog had been resting in another room, but as they walked Jude toward the end of the hall, he saw that a crowd had gathered outside the door. The entire group was milling around, all trying to look through the small window into the room. Loud sounds of things crashing were coming from inside.

"What's going on?" Dr. Powers yelled.

"That dog wants out," one of the women called back.

Jude knew he had to get him out of there before he owed them redecoration expenses as well as just the bill for veterinary services.

He was allowed to the front of the crowd, and when he looked into the window found his "wolf" pacing back and forth in the tiny room. He looked formidable as he charged the door and banged it. Had it been other than metal, it would have come down already under his weight and the power he was exerting over it. On his feet with his teeth bared, lips pulled back, head down, ears flattened against the top of his head, he looked like he belonged in a nightmare or a horror movie. If his eyes glowed red, he would look just like a werewolf. The thought was not comforting. Jude turned sideways to look at the doctor.

Dr. Powers frowned deeply. "Okay, so in all seriousness, if he comes at you, we're probably going to have to put him down. He's much too big and dangerous for us to let you walk out of here with him if he can't be controlled."

"So you were kidding before."

"I wasn't kidding about him killing you if he decides he wants to, but I was kidding about letting you just take him home. I won't actually allow you to put yourself in danger because you feel some compulsion to save his life. If he won't respond to you, we're going to euthanize him." Looking back in the window at him and then across the room to the other door, Jude saw men on the other side waiting to enter. He heard a walkie-talkie chirp behind him as Dr. Powers told the men to wait to go in until Jude did.

"Okay, Jude." She sighed, and he felt her hand on his shoulder. "Go in and see if your friend there realizes that you're his guardian angel. My guys will go in at the exact same time. If he charges you, we're going to tranquilize him."

It was like a safari instead of the back of the animal shelter, Jude thought. "I bet you had no idea tonight when you came into work that the graveyard shift was going to be so eventful."

She shrugged. "It's always something here, but yeah, this has been memorable for sure."

Jude coughed. "Just go in, huh?"

"You're stalling." Dr. Powers chuckled. "Now ready on three––in you go."

Gulping in air, he opened the door. It took only a second for the dog to recognize him. His head lifted, the snarling stopped, and the aggressive stance relaxed. He even tipped his head sideways as he looked at Jude the way dogs did.

"Hey buddy." Jude smiled at him, dropping down to one knee. "You remember me? I smell like someone you know?" Jude noticed that the dog's eyes had no white on the edges; they were just black. It was a little weird. "You wanna come home with me?"

In response the animal moved fast. Had he wanted to hurt him, no dart from a gun would have saved Jude's life. One moment the dog was across the room, the next second he was right in front of the man, inches from his face, easily able tear his throat out if that had been his desire. Jude remained frozen as the dog looked him over and then laughed when he ran his wet nose up under his chin, bumped his head up with his muzzle, and licked the base of his throat. Jude grabbed him, buried his hands in his coat, and stroked the silky fur. He was rough with his petting, and the whimper he got in response made him smile.

"Oh yeah," Dr. Powers said, and when Jude looked up at her from the floor, he found her smiling. "He definitely remembers you."

Jude buried his face in the dog's neck, unable not to, and was pleased to find that his fur smelled like pine and freshly cut wood. "He smells great. Whatever you guys washed him with smells really good."

"We didn't bathe him." She chuckled. "But I noticed that too. He smells wonderful, and that's why I'm telling you: he belongs to someone. Don't fall so in love with him that you don't put an ad in the paper. Somebody's missing him right now."

He stood up, his hand still on his dog, stroking his silky head. "Not a chance. I will find this guy's owner, believe me." The dog lifted his nose into Jude's hand and licked him before rubbing his ears against Jude's palm.

"Aww," Amy cooed as she stepped in beside the vet. "Look… he's just crazy about you. He must know you saved him."

Jude doubted that. "No, he's just checking to see if I taste like chicken or beef."

She giggled, and Jude pulled out his wallet and passed her his Visa.

"Ring him up."

Chapter Two

IT WAS hard to get a cab when you had a wolf for a companion. No one stopped, and so Jude was stuck walking through spooky neighborhoods at five in the morning. He wasn't worried though. No reason to be.

He noticed it once and thought it was just a coincidence. The ninth time it happened and was so obvious that even he couldn't miss it, he understood. People were actually crossing the street to not have to walk by him and his dog the size of a Great Dane with the head of a bear. Anyone in their right mind would run. Except Jude. Jude hadn't run. But lately he hadn't been anywhere near his right mind.

It had started at a dinner a month ago. The new director of the office, Colton Bale, had wanted to introduce his new staff to the one he had brought with him from San Francisco. Now that we were just another division of Sheridan Grant, the plan was for everyone to become one big happy family. It had never been an option for Jude, as his new boss had taken an instant liking to his boyfriend, Tiernan Saunders.

Colton had come to the table and met everyone, and when Jude had introduced his partner to him, Colton had smiled wide and taken his hand. Instantly Jude had been uncomfortable. No matter what Tiernan had said to him later in the cab, the look had been way more than just nice.

"He was interested in you," Jude had told him that night when they got home.

"You're high," Tiernan had said from the bedroom. "He's just a nice guy."

"No, he—"

"And really hot, I might add," Tiernan had teased, leaning out the door so he could see him. "Holy shit, Jude, why didn't you tell me that your new boss was mouthwateringly delicious?"

Jude had growled at him, which had sent Tiernan into peals of laughter.

"Come to bed. I wanna do bad things to you."

But there had been no heat in Tiernan's words or eyes. He had been distracted, and Jude had known he wasn't imagining it even though he had kept his worry to himself. It was stupid to accuse someone of being attracted to someone else if you didn't want to push them away. And Jude hadn't wanted Tiernan Sanders to go anywhere. They had just moved in together after a year and a half of dating, and having finally made that commitment, his plan had been to keep Tiernan around forever. And even though Jude had known Tiernan's reputation as a player, he had thought that maybe he was the one who could get him to settle down. Maybe he was the guy Tiernan had been looking for all his life. Maybe the two of them together had the potential for greatness. And it had been great, for a whole six months more.

The relationship had lasted a total of two years by the time Colton had slithered into their garden of Eden, but the ending had still outweighed all the rest. Jude could never think of the good times without the cheating that had concluded it.

When he'd gotten home early on that Friday and found Tiernan in bed with his new boss, somehow Jude hadn't been as shocked as he should have been. The late night calls Tiernan had received, the sudden concern about where his cell phone was at all times, the way Jude had never been allowed to touch it, the new password on Tiernan's laptop, they were all signs that Jude had seen but not confronted Tiernan about. Jude had known, just known, that Tiernan had been sleeping with someone; he just hadn't known it was his boss.

But it made sense to some degree. Colton made a lot of money and had a lot of things, and he looked like a movie star with his height, his build, his blond hair, and dark blue eyes. Tiernan Sanders was similarly endowed. He was model-perfect with his thick dirty-blond hair and huge emerald green eyes. The man was gorgeous and he knew it; when Jude had found them together in his bed it was more *of course* than anything else. When Tiernan had followed him out to the kitchen, he hadn't been able to look at him. It had been two weeks from the time of the dinner, and when he asked how long it had been going on, Tiernan said that they had slept together the following night after their initial meeting. The connection had been instant; they had consummated their passion while Jude was stuck in HR training. It was ironic, and as Jude had grabbed his things, he had promised Tiernan he would be out the following day. He hadn't looked back. Later that night, he had called some friends from the bar where he was drinking, and they had helped him move out of the apartment and out of his office the following day.

So in the span of a month, Jude Shea had gone from being gainfully employed and involved in a relationship to out of work and man-less. His friends had cautioned him against quitting, telling him instead to stick it out at Sheridan Grant until he found a new job, but there was no way he could look at Colton every day, knowing that Colton was sleeping with the man who used to be his. It was way too much to ask. But finding a job without having one was hard, and without being able to explain why he left, everyone thought he was a flake. For the two weeks he had been searching, he still had no leads. And now he had a dog. His life seemed to be going in the opposite direction of productive.

Finally turning onto his street, he saw his building at the other end. At the stoop that led up to the front door, he stopped and stared. The cold nose in the palm of his hand reminded him that he was not alone.

"Hey," Jude said, sitting down so that the dog and he were eye to eye. "So, look, I dunno how long we're gonna be together, and I promise I'm gonna do all I can to get you back to where you belong, but for now do you wanna hang out with me? Would that be all right?"

The dog's eyes were fixed on Jude's. Having never had a dog, Jude had no idea how you communicated with one. He'd seen it on TV and in movies, but that was about it. So since he didn't really know, he was talking to him like he would anyone else.

"I gotta call you something, so how about Joe? Not for nothing, but it was the name of my best friend when I was ten. I probably should have kept in touch with him."

Jude's dog shoved his wet nose in his eye before he licked his chin.

"Just don't eat me in the middle of the night." Jude yawned before he got back up and climbed the stairs to the front door. He was exhausted by the time he climbed the other three flights to where he lived. The old freight elevator wasn't used before eight in the morning; it was way too loud.

Inside his apartment, Jude gave his new pet the guided tour. He pointed to where the bathroom was, showed him the bedroom and that behind the screen was where the kitchen was. He went on to explain that the warmest place in the apartment was in front of the radiator that sounded like it burped when it turned on. When it made the wet gurgling noise, Joe growled, bristling with anger.

Jude laughed at him, and after a minute, Joe looked up, wagging his tail and looking, to Jude, almost embarrassed. "Haven't you ever lived inside, boy?"

All he got was a nose in the palm of his hand.

Jude made breakfast for himself and opened up two cans of wet food the vet had given him for Joe. His omelet must have smelled better, because Joe wanted nothing to do with what was in his bowl and everything to do with what Jude was eating. Since he figured eggs and ham and onions and cheese wouldn't hurt him, Jude made an omelet for the dog as well and poured him some milk to go with it. They ate together; Joe on the floor beside the stove and Jude sitting on the counter. He didn't have a table and chairs yet. It wasn't in his budget. When he collapsed on the couch a half hour later, all his energy now diverted to digesting his food, Joe stretched out on the floor beside him. Jude fell asleep with his hand on his dog's back trying to remember what it was that he was supposed to be doing on Saturday.

HIS phone woke him three hours later, and as he staggered into his bedroom, something moved out of the corner of his eye. He yelled before he remembered he had a dog.

"Shit," he gasped, his heart beating a mile a minute. He was such an idiot.

When he reached his phone he saw three missed messages from his friend Dean.

"Oh crap," he groaned, remembering suddenly that he was supposed to be helping him out with a corporate event. A month ago, when he agreed, it had seemed like no big deal to be there. Faced now with being somewhere when he was barely awake, it was harder to shower and change than he thought. When he emerged from his bathroom, he was suddenly of great interest to his dog. As he sat on the couch to put on his Converse sneakers, Joe started smelling him. The wet nose went behind his ear, down the side of his neck, and under the collar of his shirt. Jude shoved him away because it tickled.

"Personal space, buddy." Jude chuckled, pushing Joe away for the second time, digging his hands into the dog's fur as a tongue flicked out across his nose and mouth. "Gross."

At the door, he realized Joe was right beside him.

"No, buddy," Jude told him, barring him from going outside with a leg across the exit. "There are gonna be a lot of people there you don't know, and I can't have you scaring anyone."

Joe's low whine made Jude look at him.

After several moments of staring, Jude rolled his eyes and pointed to the coffee table, where the thick leather collar and leash the vet had given him were. "If we go, you gotta wear all that crap. You can't be out without it."

And amazingly Joe padded over to the table, grabbed both in his mouth, and brought them back to him. He sat still at Jude's feet and waited for him to do something. The man wondered if the action was normal even as he fit the collar over the dog's head.

"You don't talk do you?"

He just got a head tip in response.

THE event was at a campground outside the city, and by the time Jude got there, in wild disarray. In a matter of thirty minutes, everything was back on track. It was what Dean Sherwood had always most admired about his friend, Jude's seemingly innate ability to remain calm when faced with chaos and to make everyone stop and listen to him. There was no one the man couldn't work with, and no one who could remain aloof from him. Everyone liked him almost immediately, and people tended to accept his ideas and suggestions where from others they would not. When Jude snapped out orders, he did so playfully, cheerfully, his voice forever with a lilt of laughter to it and the smile that lit his eyes like a reward. Dean had wanted Jude there because it was like insurance that the event would be seamless. He'd panicked when Jude had been late.

About four in the afternoon, Jude finally took a moment to breathe and eat, sitting down on a folding chair, his burger on one side of his plate, Joe's on the other. When someone cleared their throat, he looked up and found a woman smiling down at him.

"Hi." He squinted up at her.

She pointed at Joe. "You know you really shouldn't let him eat that. He could get really sick."

Jude looked at his dog as Joe leaned forward, turned his head, and with just his tongue, in a very delicate maneuver, took the last bite of Jude's chili burger out of his fingers and swallowed it. "You want some water now?"

The dog didn't bark; he grunted his agreement. Jude wasn't sure Joe even could bark. He used the pop-top on the bottle and squirted a gentle stream of water into the dog's mouth before lifting his head to look back up at the lady giving him nutrition advice.

"Was there chili on that?" She chuckled.

He waggled his eyebrows at her.

The smile she gave him was wide as she held out her hand for him. "I'm Cecilia Benning. Who are you?"

After Jude explained that he was just the help, she took a seat on the other side of him. As soon as Cecilia was seated, Joe rose, walked around in front of her and looked at her. He didn't jump at her or put a paw on her or even get close enough to touch her. His examination was purely visual; he didn't even sniff her. Apparently that was a big deal, because she marveled over the fact that he did not seem at all like other dogs.

"May I pet him?"

"Sure."

When she reached for him, only then did Joe move close enough so she could touch him. "Jesus, he's well trained." Cecilia looked at Jude. "How long have you had him?"

"A while," he lied. He could have sworn Joe gave him a raised eyebrow. Jude scowled back at him and received a lick on his chin before the dog moved suddenly closer and got behind his ear with his tongue. Jude shoved him back, laughing, but he was like a wall of solid muscle. The whimper before his nose grazed Jude's collarbone made him smile.

"He sure loves you."

"This dog does not understand personal space at all," Jude told her as he sank his hands into the lush fur, stroking Joe's ears and scratching them.

"He understands mine," Cecilia assured him. "I think it's just yours he's missing."

Jude grunted, just like his dog.

Her laughter was warm. "I told you my name. What's yours?"

His head snapped up. "Did I not... aw, crap, I'm sorry," he said, extending his hand for her to shake. "I'm Jude Shea."

Cecilia squinted at him as she held his hand. "Why do I know that name?"

"I have no idea."

"Jude, Jude... it's not all that com... oh!" Her face lit up, and she squeezed his hand tight. "You're my sister's advertising guy! You're the one she's been looking for!"

"Who's your sister?"

"Gracie Everett."

Jude sat back, and Joe slipped in closer to him, between his thighs so that Jude's legs were on either side of the dog. "Gracie Everett. She owns Snap Dragon software."

"Yes." She grinned at Jude, standing up. "And sled dogs. She has a team that runs the Iditarod every year. She'll be thrilled to see your dog and even more so to see you. Come with me."

Since all that was left to do at the event was to coordinate the cleanup and because it was absolutely imperative to not look a gift horse in the mouth when the universe was finally giving you a break, Jude got up to go along. There were white tents set up for VIP guests, and Jude followed Cecilia to one of the larger ones.

Grace Everett looked nothing like her sister. Whereas Cecilia was tall and lithe and graceful, Gracie was short and curvy and moved erratically. She talked fast and made most people so frantic that it was hard for them to think. On Jude, she had the exact opposite effect. He felt calm in her presence, and she in his. When she saw him, she let out such a squeal of delight that she startled those standing around her. He watched her fly across the room to reach him, throwing her arms around his neck to squeeze him tight before she leaned back and stared up at him.

Gracie was almost as crazy about the man's face as she was about his mind. "Oh Jude, I found you!"

She was always struck by how delicate his features were. His eyes were huge and brown and framed with long thick lashes; his nose was small and turned up at the end, one that women paid thousands of dollars for, he had been genetically gifted with. His lips were full and pink, and he had high cheekbones and gorgeous dimples. He was truly a beautiful man, and what she found most alluring about him was that he had no idea whatsoever. The man had not been raised to trade on his looks but instead to bank on his brain. Gracie liked that. She liked it a lot.

"I found him," Cecilia corrected her sister's earlier statement. "Make sure you don't forget it."

And Jude was suddenly standing in the eye of a hurricane. Grace grabbed his hand, yanked him over to a white linen-covered table, and sat him down.

"Oh Jude, I have so much to—ohmygod, what a beautiful dog!"

And with that, Gracie was all over Joe, petting him, stroking him, telling him how gorgeous he was and how well behaved. She asked a million questions about him that Jude didn't get a chance to answer before she was back on the topic of him and why had he not been calling her back? Why on earth wasn't he returning her phone calls?

"But I don't work at Sheridan Grant anymore," he told her. "I sent out an e-mail to all my clients before I left."

Gracie looked confused. "Colton didn't say a word to me about that."

"When was the last time you saw him?"

"I don't know maybe twenty minutes ago—Sheridan Grant is one of the sponsors of this event, you know." Gracie looked at him sideways.

No, he hadn't known, and Dean, *that shit*, had neglected to tell him.

"I think that—oh, here he is now."

His head turned and there, much to his regret, was Colton Bale. He crossed quickly to Jude, looking flustered, raking his fingers through his hair before he stopped in front of him.

"Jude," Colton said breathlessly like he had run. "I thought I saw you."

Jude would not air his dirty laundry in front of one of his past clients; he was far too professional for that. There was no choice but to stand there.

"Could you step outside with me for just a minute?"

Again, there was no choice.

"Come right back, Jude," Grace called over to him. "I want you to have dinner with me, and if you don't work for Mr. Bale anymore, then we need to have a talk."

As Jude stepped outside, he felt a cool slide of silky fur against his hand and a comforting weight at his hip. Joe had moved fast to remain at his side.

"Jesus, Jude, what the hell is that?" Colton asked nervously, his eyes wide as he regarded the huge animal.

"My dog," he answered, his voice lowering.

After a long moment where Colton stared at Jude as much as he did the dog, he smiled at his former employee. "He's gorgeous. I didn't even know you had a dog."

Like the man knew anything at all about him. "I never had one before." Tiernan had hated dogs... and cats and anything you had to take care of. Even fish were a no-no. It should have been a warning sign. "He's a new addition."

"May I... is it all right if I touch him?"

Jude just shrugged. It wouldn't be his fault if Joe took the man's finger off at the knuckle. But when Colton reached for Joe, the dog turned his head like he couldn't be bothered. Jude's ex-boss came up short, touching air instead of silky, pine-scented fur.

Colton chuckled. "It looks like he doesn't like me either."

"What can I do for you?" It was hard to keep the ice out of his voice, but he tried.

"Do you remember the Ryder account?" Colton asked, clearing his throat.

"Sure."

The cough came out even though Colton tried to contain it. "Well, it seems that Belinda Ryder wants you—period. Because you worked for us at the time that you pitched the ideas to them, if you go to them without us, you're in breach of contract. But if you were to return, it would be the best-case scenario for everyone involved."

Jude wasn't sure he was hearing what he was hearing. "You've gotta be kidding."

Colton looked pained and uncomfortable. "I know how it looks, but I didn't want you to quit, Jude. I had other... plans for you that got derailed with everything else."

When Jude looked at him, his deep, dark brown eyes focused and unwavering, it was almost physically painful for Colton. The humiliation he felt, the embarrassment, it was all he could do not to squirm. The last time he had laid eyes on Jude was the day Jude discovered him in bed with his boyfriend. Colton had heard the sharp intake of breath, turned, and seen Jude standing in the doorway, staring at him and Tiernan. Once he collected himself, he had risen from the bed to speak to Jude, only to be informed by Tiernan that his colleague was gone. Colton had thought to apologize the following day at work, but Jude never gave him the opportunity, instead tendering his resignation without benefit of a two week notice. Initially happy that he would not have to face Jude again, Colton soon realized what the lapse in judgment had cost him, both personally and professionally.

It turned out that everyone both above and below Colton on the food chain at Sheridan Grant thought very highly of Mr. Judah Lee Shea. His departure had been a terrible loss, and trying to hide from clients the fact that the man was gone—even with Colton having stopped Jude's resignation e-mail from being sent out—was getting more and more difficult. Colton needed to get Jude back to work as soon as possible. His boss, the owner and CEO of the company, Nick Sheridan, had actually given him one more week to either accomplish the feat or tender his own resignation.

You didn't take over a new office and lose your biggest asset. It was not good business to drive away the top producer, the man who generated more revenue than anyone else. Colton had been tasked by his boss with returning Jude to the fold immediately. He was told to offer whatever sum of money or perform whatever amount of groveling Jude deemed necessary.

"I never meant for you to leave Jude," he repeated quickly with a flashing smile. "My reputation is just shot and… everyone knows, you know?" The inter-office e-mail was full of rumor and innuendo, teeming with wild speculation about what exactly Colton Bale had done to beloved, respected, and talented Jude to make him quit. The glances he got, the way no one ever looked him in the eye, the whispering that went on behind his back, and how silent a room became when he entered… it was all exhausting, and he was sick of it. He had let his little head think for his big one and was paying the price for a gross error in judgment.

"Hello?"

"Sorry." Colton cleared his throat, his eyes flicking back to Jude's big brown ones. And how in the hell had he been so blind? All he had seen was the blond beauty that was Tiernan Saunders, and when the smoke cleared, he had so had completely missed that Jude was the real find. He was smart and funny and sexy… *God, he was sexy*… and when he smiled…. Colton actually pictured the smile when he jerked off lately. He imagined all sorts of scenarios that would direct the smile his way, imagined Jude naked under him most of all.

Everything was such a mess, and there didn't seem any way to fix it.

"Are you all right?" Jude asked.

Colton took a breath, calming his racing heart, trying not to think about the blood rushing to his groin. "Listen, Mr. Sheridan, he wants to see you when he's in town for the meeting with Ryder on Monday."

Jude just stared at the man, absolutely certain that Colton Bale had lost his mind.

"I left you at least twenty messages on your phone, and I've emailed you, and- and I know that this thing between me and you and Tiernan is—"

"My phone automatically deletes anything from you."

Colton nodded, smiling sheepishly. "Okay, but now that I'm standing here in front of you, would you consider coming back? If this all goes well, you can write your own ticket, and definitely you won't have to report to me. Natalie Torres is the new East Coast Marketing Director. You would report to her. She'll be here Monday as well."

Jude squinted at him.

"What?"

"Did you tell them I would show up?"

"I might have."

Jude nodded. "And what was your plan to get me there?"

The heavy sigh rose out of Colton. "I didn't actually have one. I figured you watching me getting my head handed to me might appeal to you."

"It might," Jude agreed.

"Can I interest you in a raise?" Colton smiled at him, hoping he'd take the bait.

Jude crossed his arms over his chest. "You have all my notes for that proposal; you don't actually need me."

Colton nodded, looking away from him and then back. "Here's the thing. The client trusts you to not screw her vision, because you were the one who listened to her and came up with the concept to begin with. She thinks you're the only one who *gets* her, and so her faith rests in the relationship with you and not with the firm."

"And so, what? If not for the client, I wouldn't have ever heard from you?"

Colton's eyes were back on Jude's. "It's not just that client. There's Mrs. Everett back in the tent who wants to offer you a job, and Tom Youngblood, and Scott Ames… the list goes on. You're brilliant, Jude, and you know it, and all your clients trust you like nothing I've ever seen. You filter ideas and see things much faster than the rest of us. The problem is that you're such a self-righteous prick about it. If I could drill some humility into you, we'd be all set."

Jude knew that about himself: he had to be right. He had a lousy personal self-image and an inflated ego when it came to his work. He was a pain in the ass to figure out, which was why his circle of friends had always been so small and tight.

"I need you, Jude, but you need us too. Having a reputation as brilliant but unmanageable is not designed to get you lots of job offers. There are a lot of mundane thinkers who can accept critique and criticism with much more secure futures than yours."

At which point, Jude was going to tell Colton Bale to go to hell, but his dumb dog shoved his nose in his hand. Jude told himself that he had to think about the dog, and so sucking it up and swallowing his pride was in order. It was hard to feed a wolf when you had no money. Not that he was in a bad place yet, his savings was still keeping him off the street, but he did not want to completely deplete his safety net.

"Well?" Colton asked.

"What time on Monday?"

Colton could not stop the relieved sigh or the unguarded smile "They're coming at ten. Be in my office at nine, all right? I'll messenger over contracts to you tomorrow morning. You call me if anything at all doesn't sound right or fair."

Jude nodded.

"Everyone wants you back. The entire team has been in turmoil since you left. They all want you as creative director. Mr.

Sheridan's prepared to give you that title and have you report to Torres, like I said."

Jude gave no outward sign of the elation he felt inside.

"Okay?" Colton pressed.

"Okay."

"Great," Colton breathed out, his smile huge as he looked at Jude's face and then at Joe. "Can I pet the dog now, maybe?"

Jude turned and looked down at Joe. "Whaddya say, boy? Throw the man a bone?"

In response, Joe stepped forward and lifted his muzzle to Colton. The man knelt down in front of Jude's pet and buried his hands in the thick coat.

"God, he's gorgeous, when did you get him?"

"Last night."

"Last night?" Colton chuckled, smiling up at Jude, unable to keep his eyes from trailing back down the man to his groin "You're kidding?"

Jude shook his head.

Colton made sure he took a breath before he rose from his crouch in front of the dog so he could breathe and talk at the same time. How could he have been so stupid? He was never wrong and he never, ever leaped before looking, but Tiernan was gorgeous, so gorgeous in fact, that Colton hadn't even seen Jude. Tiernan was so hot that Colton never stopped to ask who the top was and who was the bottom. And while it was true that Tiernan Saunders was versatile, he had a definite preference, and that preference was all that Colton Bale was. Never in his life had Colton bottomed for anyone, and he was not about to start for Tiernan Saunders just because he was hot.

When the arguments started and the frustration rose, the truth about Jude had come out. Before they ended their short affair, Tiernan had told Colton the many things that Jude had allowed him to do to him in bed. The idea of Jude being tied up, held down, and begging nearly undid him. Colton had not been able to get the pictures out of his head since. Faced with the man, it was hard to meet his gaze.

"Okay, so, Monday."

Colton came out of his fog and realized that Jude was already walking away from him.

"Wait, I wanted you to have dinner with me, and—"

"Nope, I've got plans. I'll see ya."

Colton cleared his throat, reaching out to touch the younger man, to keep him there, talking. "Just so you know… Tiernan and I… that's over."

Jude leaned just out of his reach so Colton had no choice but to let him go.

"Yeah, he, um… we didn't…we don't… anyway, just so you know. It's not like if you see me, you'll see him," Colton tried to explain.

"Okay."

"It wasn't what either of us thought."

Jude had no idea what that meant, but neither did he have any interest in asking.

"Wait," Colton said, unable not to sound pleading as he jogged over to Jude. He had to take a step back, though, when Joe was suddenly barring his path. "Huh, he's very protective for one day."

Jude shrugged. "He seems to like me."

"I did—do, too, Jude, I just got distracted."

What did that even mean? "Yeah, okay, I'll see ya," Jude said before he turned to walk back toward Mrs. Everett's tent.

Colton had to go in the opposite direction. He had people waiting for him. There was no reason for him to stay. "Monday at nine, Jude," Colton called after the man he wanted to take home with him in the worst way.

Jude waved to let him know he'd heard him but didn't turn around. He was exhilarated and overwhelmed at the same exact time. In one day his life had gone from scary to solid. It was hard to process. Before he rejoined Mrs. Everett, he called his friend Taylor to tell him the good news that he was back to being employed and to accept the invitation to a party he had declined earlier in the week. Since he now had something to celebrate, Jude would show up along with everyone else to get his drink on. It was Saturday night, after all.

Chapter Three

JUDE took his dog and left the event as soon as the swag—the gift bags—was handed out. Leaving the cleanup to Dean's minions, he drove directly to the liquor store. He was surprised that the store owner didn't say a word to him about Joe, instead giving the dog a pat over the top of the counter. It was funny how people were either scared or hypnotized by Joe. Mrs. Everett had been unable to keep her hands off him, and even Colton had been riveted. At Taylor's the reaction from his friends was unanimous; they thought Joe was awesome. The problem was that their interest in him translated into feeding him food off their plates, filling bowls with beer, and, in Jude's friend Kara's case, braiding his big scary beast a garland of ribbons. Everyone said he looked like some mythical creature with it draped around his neck.

"You look like an idiot," Jude assured him as he sat on the back porch with his legs stretched out on the railing in front of him. "They're just lying to you so you don't feel like such a dork."

The look he got back suggested a pot-to-kettle comment in return. It was funny that in the course of a day Jude had started thinking for his dog. There was a name for that, giving animals human thoughts and emotions, but after many shots of Cuervo with Corona chasers, there was no way to drag it from his mental Rolodex.

It was Saturday night, and so by eleven there was a full house. There were people crowding the front and back porches, the front and back lawns, spilling out on all sides, in every room, especially the living room where the music was. Jude was dancing, and though normally he was more inhibited and so saved his dirty dancing for the privacy of his own home, because he was drunk and feeling good, he just let go. His body moved like it was liquid, and a lot of men and women noticed. Finally, when he couldn't take watching him anymore, Taylor Gossett yanked him off the floor, dragged him through the crowd to the kitchen, and shoved him up against the wall by the back door.

"What the hell are you doing?" Taylor demanded.

"Whaddya mean?"

He wedged his knee between Jude's thighs. "If you're looking to get laid, I will scratch that itch for you, my friend."

Jude smiled slyly, looking at him through narrowed eyes. "Is that right?"

Taylor nodded slowly. "You have no idea what you look like; you never have."

"What do I look like?" Jude teased, one eyebrow arching provocatively.

Taylor's eyes locked on Jude's. "You're like the hottest guy here, Jude, and you don't even know it."

Jude gave a deep sigh before he flattened his hands on Taylor's chest. "Show me."

"Goddamn," Taylor breathed out, his hand sliding up Jude's throat. "You have this amazing body and your skin is… and those big brown eyes… shit, you never notice the guys that trip all over themselves just to try and talk to you."

He was so full of shit. Jude knew his ex had been the beautiful one. Jude was built like a swimmer with long lean, sinewy muscles. He wasn't perfection like Tiernan was; there were flaws with him. "Okay," he said, patronizing him.

"Jude," Taylor snapped, "baby, you are seriously hot, seriously traffic-stopping gorgeous. The fact that you don't know it, don't use it… that just makes it even hotter."

Jude grinned evilly. "And so what? Put up or shut up."

Taylor smiled back at Jude, shaking his head. "Don't tease."

"Who's teasing?"

"Do you have any idea how bad I wanna take you to bed?"

"Fine," Jude drawled, leaning into Taylor. "Take me to bed, pound me into the floor."

"Fuck," Taylor said reverently at the same time the bloodcurdling snarl froze them both.

Jude snorted out a laugh. Damn dog and his shitty timing.

Taylor had an altogether different reaction. He gasped and shoved Jude off him, retreating several feet away. "What the fuck, Jude?"

Jude looked down and found his dog there, hair raised, lips drawn back over sharp fangs, looking like he was fresh from running across the tundra. The kitchen had gone silent, and no one moved because Joe was *that* scary.

Jude smiled sheepishly, staggered to the back door, threw it open, and stumbled out onto the patio. Flopping down onto the lawn chair, Joe was right there with his nose in his eye. Jude laughed so hard the tears rolled down his cheeks.

"You asshole." Jude could barely breathe. "How the fuck am I supposed to get laid with you thinking you're protecting me?"

JOE, who was aware of both the words and the intent, licked the tears off Jude's cheeks, the base of his throat, and the sensitive skin behind his ears. As a man, he could have done something about the feelings that surged tirelessly through him; but as a dog, as Joe, he could not.

In his present form, as Joe, he could only protect the fragile human even though he wanted to do much more. He longed to show Jude Shea the vast difference between being loved by a man and being loved by a man who was his soul's mate. Because Jude was his heart, because the clueless young man belonged to him, Joe, in his dog form, would allow no other in Jude's bed. He would slaughter anyone who tried.

Colton Bale had been lucky to walk away with his life earlier in the day; the scent of arousal had rolled off the man so heavily that Joe had been surprised Jude didn't smell it. Not that Jude seemed to notice any of the men—or women—who were interested in him. And that was fine. He liked Jude oblivious; it made him happy. The only thing better would be Jude begging, Jude under him writhing in drowning, throbbing pleasure, head thrown back, eyes closed, his spine bowed, panting out his name… Eoin. Yes, that would be better, and it was going to happen very, very soon.

Eoin Thral knew he couldn't take much more of the man's delicious, intoxicating scent, his gentle hands on him, or the enticing warmth of his skin. Eoin had never thought that he would find his *cairn*, the heart of a guardian, but now that he had discovered him, had found Jude Shea, he couldn't imagine his life without him.

Jude Shea belonged to him. Jude had felt the pull to find Eoin, and in that process, had saved his life… literally. Eoin couldn't have fought the three gryphons much longer; he had lost too much blood and he was on the wrong side of the veil to heal so much damage. But just when he thought he was done, his angel had appeared.

Eoin had seen him, had watched, powerless to do anything to stop it, as Jude stood his ground as the others bore down on him. He was then overcome with joy and relief when the other humans arrived. The attacking gryphons had no alternative but to retreat or risk exposure. Left alone, Eoin had resigned himself to his death until he had felt the pulse deep within him, the throb of awakening, of recognition.

This was his heart he was looking at, his *cairn* who tenderly lifted his head and cradled it in his lap. This was his mate, who spoke soft words meant to soothe and reassure him. The man who pressed his face close to his, whose scent filled his chest with longing and sent hot blood rushing to his groin, hardening his cock. This man he would hold forever in the circle of his arms and never let go. As soon as Eoin lured Jude through the veil, he could transform back into a man and claim him. In Jude's world Eoin was a dog, as all guardians were who had not claimed a mate, but in his, in Midrin, he was a man, and Jude would be his. He simply had to figure out a way to coax his mate through the veil.

"Are you listening to me?" Jude laughed hard, dragging Eoin's thoughts back from where they had been: in bed… with Jude. "Big dumb dog, quit licking me! It's gross. Dog slobber is totally disgusting." Jude could have sworn the dog looked at him indignantly, which sent him into new peals of laughter.

"Jude?"

He looked up at his friend Taylor.

"Let's go," Taylor said.

"Go?"

"Yeah." Taylor smiled lazily. "Let's drop your dog at your place, and then lemme take you home with me."

But how could Jude leave Joe alone? That hardly seemed fair. Petting his dog before he stood up, Jude sighed heavily. "No, it's a bad idea. I like you too much to sleep with you."

"What?" Taylor was indignant.

But Jude didn't need a fuck-buddy or a one-night stand; he needed to be in bed with someone who wanted more than just hours with him. It had always been his problem. He was a total washout in the casual sex department.

"You're a goddamn cocktease, Jude! You always were!" Taylor barked at him. "And your dog is fuckin' creepy as shit."

And that was funny all over again. Sex called off on account of dog... hilarious.

Walking around the house minutes later, Jude explained to Joe about who Taylor was, about his ex-boyfriend, and about the total tragedy that was his dating life. Apparently he was much too serious and not enough fun to be in a relationship with. Monogamy was a deal-breaker for him, and that was a tough one for most guys. A lot of his friends said that he was a straight man living in a gay man's body, but he had a lot of girlfriends with cheating ex-husbands and boyfriends. It had nothing to do with homosexual or heterosexual and everything to do with basic makeup. You were either made loyal or not, and he was—end of story. Of course it was easy for Joe to understand, as all a dog could ever be was loyal. And that made Jude wonder about women who called men who ran around "dogs." How did that make any sense at all?

The walk home cleared his head, and Jude called Taylor and left him a message when he didn't pick up. He explained that he was drunk and told Taylor to pick the day and he would feed him. Any day, anytime, he just wanted them to be okay. He got a text back that they were okay, but he wanted Jude's ass, not food. But burgers would have to suffice since sex was off the table.

"What a weird day," he told his dog, who was practically dancing along at his side.

When Jude got home, he drank the water he was supposed to, took some Tylenol to head off the threatening hangover, and went in and collapsed on his bed. Minutes later, Joe was there beside him, on the floor, lifting his muzzle into Jude's hand. And as Jude's eyes fluttered shut, his dog, Joe, who was really Eoin Thral, guardian of Drelindah Holt, Baroness of Saraso, shivered under the touch of his mate's fingers in his fur.

Chapter Four

MONDAY morning at eight sharp, Jude arrived in his old office—soon to be his office again—feeling good but somehow naked without his constant companion of the last three days. It was amazing how quickly Jude had gotten used to having his pet with him. Sunday had been spent watching TV, eating takeout, and ending with a trip out for sushi. His friends Beth and Eric Hudson had never seen a dog eat a spicy Ahi roll and weren't sure he should, but since no one seemed to care, they went with it. The four of them had ice cream afterward, and since Jude did know that dogs and chocolate didn't mix, he didn't let Joe have that. Pistachio didn't seem to be a problem, however.

"That's so gross, Jude." Beth made a face as she watched Joe lick the waffle cone in his hand. "You shouldn't eat after him."

"No?" Jude looked at Joe as the dog licked behind his ear. "Why? Are nuts bad?"

"Oh, forget it." She giggled as Joe started sniffing Jude's hair, leaning on him, pushing on him until Jude relented and lay down on his back in the grass. The park at dusk was beautiful and quiet and cold. Why they were even having ice cream was beyond Jude, but it was good and so was the company. That his dog was now lazily running his nose under his chin, up and down over his throat, was funny.

And now, Monday at work, walking back into his old place of business was a little unsettling. He felt safe with his wolf at his side, and suddenly, without Joe, Jude felt the exact opposite. He was vulnerable, and he didn't like it.

As the day wore on, Jude slowly regained any lost composure. His meeting with Mr. Sheridan, the owner and CEO of the company, had gone amazingly well, and Jude had been assured that he was on track to do big things. Mr. Sheridan was invested in Jude's future and made it clear that he wanted him to stay with the company. Jude no longer reported to Colton Bale, but to Natalie Torres, the East Coast Marketing Director, and the two of them had clicked the minute she started talking. She was thrilled to have Jude on her team, and he was to meet her at her office in New York so they could go over their expectations of each other.

Until then, Jude was ordered to just take some time and relax. When he told Natalie that it was okay—he didn't need any more time off; he could start immediately—she countered with an explanation. Being on vacation where you knew you had a job waiting for you was completely different than being out of work looking for a job. He needed to take some time to clear his head and relax; she insisted on it.

Since her logic was sound and her tone final, Jude thanked his new boss profusely and went on leave after he went around the office and announced to everyone that he was back. He'd had no idea that he had even been missed. It turned out that since he had returned, several people were no longer leaving. It was illuminating for Jude to realize his importance.

"Jude?"

Looking away from his window, he found Colton in his office. Jude was surprised. "What are you… didn't we sign everything?"

Colton smiled at him. "Yes, we did."

Jude nodded. "Okay."

Colton's expression changed slowly to concern. "You all right?"

"Yeah, thanks." Jude smiled back. "So what are you doing here?"

"I just wanted to tell you that it's really good to have you back."

"Thanks," Jude said, crossing the room to him, holding out his hand. "And thanks for lookin' me up. You didn't have to, so—"

"Oh, the hell I didn't," Colton said, tightening his grip when Jude tried to pull his hand free. "Everybody wanted you back…. I wanted you back."

Jude nodded, easing his hand from Colton's. "Well, thanks again," he said evenly, walking to his desk, picking up his courier bag, and heading for the door. "I'll see ya when I get back."

"Wait."

Jude turned, doing as he was asked.

The brown eyes flicking to his made Colton Bale, high powered executive, mute.

"Colton?"

"Oh…well I was going to invite you to dinner," he forced a smile. "I just…I think that it's important for us to clear the air and be sure that from a new place of understanding that we both try and—"

"What?"

He was rambling and he knew he was rambling and there was absolutely nothing he could do to stop it. Jude Shea had him good and flustered.

"Do you want some water?" Jude asked, remembering that he had a couple of bottles stored in the break room.

"No I…I just think if we have dinner we can talk and put things behind us ya know? I mean we're gonna be colleagues and I want that to be seamless. I owe you that."

"You don't owe me anything."

But Colton knew he owed Jude a great deal. He especially owed him for being more professional than petty and being able to rise above his personal feelings to return to work. He didn't know many other men able to put aside their own pride.

"Jude I—"

"You want the transition to be seamless," Jude clarified, "and it will be."

"Jude—"

"Now if you'll excuse me, I've gotta get home and walk my dog before he tears my place apart."

"Why don't I meet you at your place, and after you take him for a walk, we can grab some dinner? I'd love to pick your brain about some things."

"When I get back." Jude smiled before he walked out and left Colton alone in his office.

Jude took a cab home instead of the subway because he was really starting to worry about what his apartment was going to look like. He was surprised when his cell phone rang as he started walking down his side street twenty minutes later.

"Mr. Shea?"

"Yes?"

"Hi, this is Amy from the animal shelter."

"Oh crap," Jude groaned. "I was supposed to do the follow-up check with the vet on Joe this morning. Shit, I totally forgot until right this—"

"No, no," she said, cutting him off. "It's fine. I just wanted to call and tell you that I think we found the dog's owner."

Jude froze; he couldn't take another step. His stomach felt like it had dropped out of his body. "What? I'm sorry what'd you say?"

"We found the dog's owner." Amy sounded so excited. "Or I should say that he found us? I mean, normally we don't get to reunite a pet with his owner like this so fast… but he came in this morning and had the description down to the details. He even knew what the dog smelled like! It was amazing. I can't wait for you to meet him, and he can't wait to meet you."

"Really." Jude felt like he was in a fog. When had the stupid dog become so important? How could he get attached to an animal that he had no business even having? He didn't work a job conducive to having a boyfriend, much less a pet.

"Yeah," Amy rambled on. "We gave him your address and phone number. But he was so thrilled to hear that his dog was in one piece; he's probably on his way over there right now."

"How did he lose him?" Jude asked.

"Well, I guess this guy—Cuyler something, it was a little hard to understand him—he uses the dog to hunt, and I guess when they were on their way back from their last trip, your dog got separated from the rest of them when they stopped to eat."

But Joe was so well trained! Why would he have run?

"So he's been just crazed for like the last three days and finally came to see us," Amy finished.

"Why did it take so long for him to check the shelter?" Jude asked faintly.

"Well, from what he said, they don't have shelters where he's from."

How was that even possible? As far as Jude knew, there were animal shelters in every city in the United States. "And where is that?"

"I dunno. Canada, maybe?"

Two men could get married in Canada, but there were no animal shelters there… bull. It was a lie, and the sinking feeling in the pit of Jude's stomach was turning into full-blown anxiety. "Okay, so when did you say he was coming?"

"I suspect he'll be there anytime. Like I said, he was excited." Amy sighed. "And normally we don't give out personal information to people like we did yours, but the description of the dog…. There's no way it's not his, and I know you had no plans to keep him. So it works out for everybody."

"Sure," Jude said, his voice devoid of emotion.

She talked for a few more minutes, but Jude was no longer listening. Just thinking about giving up Joe had his heart hurting. When he got closer to home and spotted the man sitting on the front stoop of his building, he felt his stomach roll.

"Good evening," the stranger said as he stood. "Are you Jude Shea?"

Jude nodded, swallowing hard. "Yes."

The man's smile was fast, but it didn't hit his eyes. In fact, the pale blue eyes were cold and flat. The man was tall and handsome in a way that conjured up thoughts of Vikings and old Norse gods. Jude could believe that the man was a hunter and that Joe was his dog; they looked like they belonged together. What did the creative director of a PR firm need with a dog that would be at home in a cabin in the woods bringing down elk or moose or whatever else?

A hand was held out to him. "Would you be having my dog, Mr. Shea?"

Jude nodded, taking the offered hand.

His fingers curled around Jude's, shaking his hand hard. "The woman at the shelter spoke to me that without your help that Eoin would be dead... I thank ye for your compassion."

But he didn't say it like he meant it. Jude heard only words; there was no feeling behind them. The speech was rehearsed, and that knowledge combined with Jude's feelings of loss and anxiety from earlier became all-out suspicion. Who was this guy, and what did he want with Joe?

"I am needing Eoin back as I am unable return without him."

"What's the dog's name?"

"Eoin."

"Sounds like something out of *Lord of the Rings*." Jude forced a smile.

There was no instant agreement, no laughter... the man had no idea what Jude was talking about, had no frame of reference for either the Tolkien classic or Peter Jackson's epic. How was that even possible?

"May I see him?" The man pressed him, taking a step forward.

Jude tested the water. "You must have been just sick about losing him,"

"Aye, might I see him?"

Jude nodded. "He's a real sweet dog."

The man was surprised, and before he could suppress it, Jude saw it all over his face.

"You disagree?"

He shrugged. "He is a hunting dog, Mr. Shea—a guard dog. Sweet is not what I would call him."

"Okay." Jude retreated, taking a step back. "Maybe since I'm off tomorrow, I could—"

"Please," he pleaded, closing the distance between them quickly, abruptly invading Jude's personal space. "Make me not wait." His accent was strange, as well as the way he put the words together. "I will follow you." It was a statement, not a question.

"No." Jude's tone left no room for argument. "I'll bring him down."

"Mr. Shea, you—"

"No," Jude repeated, his voice hardening. "I will bring him down."

He nodded slowly, looking him over. "As you say."

Turning, Jude headed up the stoop.

"Mr. Shea."

Looking back down at him, Jude realized that even from where he was, above him, the man still looked big. He was tall and thick; linebacker size, easily between six-three and six-five with broad shoulders and a wide chest, built like a refrigerator with a head. If he wanted to hurt Jude, he could.

"Do not run, Jude Shea, for I will catch you."

Jude squinted down at him. "I'm sorry I didn't catch your name."

The man took the steps up to Jude fast, scary fast for so large a man, and stood between him and the safety of his building. "I gave you not my name, veiler, but it is Cuyler Adon, gryph of the royal house of Paradoon."

And suddenly Jude was in a weird place. "What's a veiler?" he asked, taking a step back.

"You," Cuyler's voice had gone icy. "You are a veiler, for you live here."

Which made no sense, but Jude let it go, deciding instantly to play the only card he had. The man knew nothing about Chicago, that was clear, so Jude used that. "So, do you have some ID I can see?"

Worry flickered across Cuyler's features, and Jude jumped on the opening.

"I mean, if you don't have ID, I can't just let you take Joe, ya know? The police won't allow it, and since we have officers in every building, even this one"—he tipped his head at the door—"we'd both be in trouble."

"You have armed men in this keep?"

Keep? "Yep," Jude lied, unsure of what the hell a keep was. "Sure do."

Cuyler nodded, his eyes narrowing, studying Jude, trying to gauge the sincerity of his words.

Jude tried to look bored; he even yawned like everything he was telling Cuyler Adon was simply understood, too mundane to even question. "So you wanna maybe come back when you've got some ID?"

"Aye," Cuyler said before he was down the stoop and back on the sidewalk. He looked back up at Jude once before he turned to stalk down the street, the stride visibly angry.

Jude was inside the apartment building fast, taking the three flights faster than he ever had. The second he opened his door, Joe rose from where he was on the rug beside the couch and bounded over to him. Dropping his bag on the floor, Jude knelt in front of him, his hands on him, stroking over the beloved face.

"Oh shit, buddy, we gotta get you out of here."

Joe pulled back from licking the base of his throat to look into Jude's eyes. Worry and fear were rolling off the man in thick waves, and Joe felt like he was drowning in emotion.

"Some guy named Cuyler Adon was just here, and he wants you bad." Instantly tense, Joe pulled back from Jude, staring into his eyes. "I'm gonna change, and then I'll figure out where I'm gonna stash ya. 'Cause seriously, that guy is no more your owner than I am."

Minutes later, in jeans and a sweater, Jude was reaching for his sneakers when Joe carried over his hiking boots.

"Now you're dressing me?" Jude smiled at him, petting Joe before he got a cold wet nose shoved in his eye. "Good for nothing dog." Jude scratched under his chin until he closed his eyes. "I missed you today."

In answer, there was a low whimper before Joe licked the side of his neck. Jude shoved him back and got up, boots laced, ready to walk out. But the dog wasn't done; he brought Jude his pea coat as well. And it was cold outside, but still, how did Joe know?

Halfway down the stairs to the front door, Joe suddenly froze, and Jude looked up. Directly in front of him, separated only by two wood and glass doors, was Cuyler Adon. And this time he had friends with him.

All three men looked just like Cuyler, eastern European and just as big. Jude saw the ax a second before the glass of the outer security door was shattered. He turned around and ran for the back door. Joe was right beside him, and as he took the five stairs to the basement, the dog brushed by him. It took precious seconds for Jude to get his keys out and open the door, but the noise as it locked behind him was very satisfying. It was a metal door, easily four inches thick, and you had to use a key to get in and a key to get out. Jude knew it would hold.

It was still scary to hear the men hit it, their combined weight making a sound like an impact tremor. Racing across the floor, he was at the other side that led up to the alley in seconds. Outside with the second door closed behind him, he took a breath before he was yanked forward. Joe had taken hold of his coat and tugged hard.

"Wait," Jude cautioned him, standing there, trying to figure out what to do.

The banging on the door behind him let him know that the men had gotten through the first door and were just minutes away from getting through the second one. He bolted across the street without a second thought.

Jude ran fast, faster than he had ever run in his life, across wet grass, through mud, only the traction from his hiking boots keeping him from slipping and falling.

"Eoin Thral!"

Jude looked over his shoulder and saw the men flying after him, arms pumping, legs driving them forward. Only then was he truly scared. His adrenaline kicked in making flight the only possibility. He had to run, had to get away, his only point of focus the dog a few yards in front of him. He had tunnel vision except for Joe. Only the yelling behind him made him turn his head and look. There were five men in all, the number having increased by two, all with only one objective… to kill Jude if he fell. There was no doubt in his mind that for whatever reason, just getting Joe wasn't enough. He had to die too.

Swerving across another street, Jude saw Joe running toward the small park behind the school. He followed blindly, knowing that beyond the park was the library. It was hard to see in the dark and the slight fog; it was lucky that he knew where he was going. He heard the slap of boots on asphalt and knew that the men were close. Speeding up, he turned around to make sure he knew where Joe was.

The dog was gone. Jude screamed his name, but he didn't appear. With how thick the fog had suddenly become, Joe could have been just steps ahead of him and Jude would have missed him. It was hard to make out anything.

Jude wanted to stop, catch his breath, and get his bearings, but he didn't dare. The men were seconds behind, and so he ran on blindly, hoping not to slam into a tree or the side of a building, surprised that he was still running over frozen grass and not pavement. The park was not that big; maybe he was running in circles.

"Lose him not; if he runs to the gate alone we are done!"

Jude had no idea who was yelling or why. He just needed to get out of the fog so he could see where he was.

"Jude!"

He turned toward the sound of his name, because it wasn't Cuyler. He knew the guttural sound of his voice already; this was someone else.

"Here!"

Pivoting to his left, Jude stopped for a second, and in that heartbeat of time, he was grabbed roughly, swung around, and yanked forward. He crashed into a man, but even with his momentum sending Jude careening into him, Jude didn't knock him down. Instead, strong arms were wrapped around him, his own pinned to his sides, as he was crushed against a hard, solid chest. Lifting his head to see who held him, Jude found dark eyes, dark hair, and lips curved into a slight smile. He caught his breath.

"Fear me not," the man said, his voice low, husky and smooth.

Jude trembled, terrified as he was instantly released and in the next moment, shoved hard to his right. Stepping back to correct his balance, his foot hit only air. The ground was no longer solid under him. His wind-milling arms accounted for nothing as he fell back. He saw the man for a second above him before he leaped after Jude.

In Jude's ears there was a steady building roar, against his face blew freezing air, and there was pressure, squeezing and pushing until there was no air to breathe and suddenly no light to see. There was only darkness and nothing else.

Chapter Five

JUDE was dreaming, and any second he was going to wake up. He would be back in his bed, back in his apartment instead of thrown over a saddle, trussed up like the prisoner he seemingly was. The whole experience had to be his very active imagination at work. There was no other logical explanation for him seeing what he was seeing: countryside instead of city streets, streams instead of a Starbucks, and a forest where buildings should have been. Even the smells were wrong, instead of gasoline and the warring aromas of food there was only the pungent fragrance of grass and earth coming sharp to his senses on the crisp evening breeze.

The grass was high along the path, brushing the sides of the horse, the road they followed barely one, more a winding dirt track along the ground. He heard insects in loud chorus only to go silent as they passed. It was almost beautiful, the stillness, the moonlight illuminating how vast the land was, only trees and brush as far as the eye could see. He would have been scared out in the open if he had been alone because for all the beauty of the scene there was also something ancient and quiet that Jude didn't like. Noises, like traffic, calmed him, soothed him, that there was only the sound of the wind through the grass, was eerie. The forest loomed beyond the clearing they were riding through and beyond that the blackness that he knew was mountains. Slung over the saddle of the horse, the only travelers on a lonely road, Jude was both uncomfortable and wary.

He had transported himself to the middle of nowhere for no reason he could fathom. Jude didn't dream about the country; he dreamed about five-star hotels and room service. Horses, the smell of leather, and sweat, pine, sandalwood, and just man… normally cologne and soap turned him on, not the whole outdoorsy thing. Most women he knew had the whole highland Scottish laird fantasy, but as an out and proud gay man, it just wasn't him. A top was one thing; uber-straight guy doing him on a pallet bed in his tent was not really his idea of a good time. He was much too pragmatic. Like, what did they do for lube in the Middle Ages?

Jude had to try and separate fact from fantasy. Had he fallen? Hit his head? Had the guys chasing him caught and killed him? Was he dead and this was hell? Being stuck in medieval times for all eternity was his punishment for whatever it was he had done? Was that possible? Fingers stroked his hair suddenly and brought his attention back to the present… *or his dream*… or his present dream. God, he really needed to wake up.

He had obviously fallen in the park and was now somewhere passed out, probably behind the library. All of it must have happened before he was grabbed. Before the man had pulled him into his arms… the man with the very sexy dark eyes… he had already been unconscious. Jude knew he must have passed out before the man appeared, because tall, dark, and gorgeous had definitely been part of his fantasy. He didn't exist; Jude had to have been already unconscious at that point. He had to be dreaming or…

maybe he was in a coma. Maybe this was what a coma was like. Maybe you dreamed without brakes, without any control at all.

Everything just felt so real. Not only could Jude see everything clearly—or as clearly as one could in moonlight—but he could smell the man whose saddle he was slung over. He could smell the man's horse as well as the wet earth and some kind of flowers. Jude was uncomfortable, and he couldn't wake up. Those were all tell-tale signs of reality. But all evidence aside, there was no way he was awake. He could not be where he thought he was, trotting down a dirt road that snaked its way through a heavily wooded area. No such place existed in downtown Chicago.

"Excuse me," he said tentatively.

The slap to his ass was immediate. It stung even through his jeans and the blanket he was wrapped in.

"Shit," Jude groaned, wiggling to try to get where the pommel of the saddle would not grind into his ribs.

"Speak not, *cairn*, or I shall be forced to bind you."

Threats? His fantasy man was threatening him? "Are you kidding? Get me down… now!"

Instantly the horse was stopped, and Jude felt himself slipping, sliding, and then falling before he hit very hard ground. His back felt like it was on fire as all the air was sucked from his lungs in an instant. He had fallen out of his bunk bed once when he was nine; it felt exactly the same, striking the floor with enough force to hurt and wind him. The difference was that instead of someone checking to make sure if he was okay, a strip of cloth was shoved between his lips, and he was roughly rolled to his stomach as the gag was tied tight behind his head.

"You were warned, *cairn*, and must now heed my words."

Heed his words? Was he high?

Rolled back over, Jude focused his eyes and looked up at the madman who apparently resided deep in his subconscious.

His scowl as he surveyed Jude fired his dark eyes. "You must be still, *cairn*, as we are not yet close to the holding, and the woods are full of danger."

It was the same guy who had grabbed him and thrown him off the cliff... or the same *dream* guy, since there was no cliff in the park and he was already asleep when that part happened. And why, beyond seeing the man before, did he seem so familiar?

He knelt down beside Jude, brushing the hair off his forehead. "Do you know me, *cairn*?"

Jude wanted to explain that his name was not "Karn" or "Kayrin" or "Karen" or whatever the guy was using besides what was on his birth certificate. But the warm hand sliding over his jaw and down the length of his throat brought his attention back to the man.

"I wanted not to bind you, *cairn*, but for your action that made it so." His smile made Jude's stomach flutter, and he had no idea why. Big muscular guys were not normally his type. He didn't like the idea of being manhandled, thrown down, and fucked hard. Jude preferred slow and gentle with a lover built more like he was, sinewy and lean.

"Look here to me."

And he talked funny.

"You will obey."

If he hadn't been gagged, Jude would have told him what he could do with his "obey" command, but because he couldn't, he just stared into the man's eyes. Jude meant to glare but ended up forgetting that he was angry as the man was in possession of the darkest, blackest, most beautiful pair of eyes he had ever seen. They were like liquid onyx, and, as he had observed the first time, sexy as hell. The rest of his face was just as stunning. He had great cheekbones, a long straight nose, and a sensuous mouth made to be kissed. The lips were full and dark, and imagining them on his cock sent slivers of heat racing through Jude. As if the man could read his mind, one perfectly shaped black eyebrow rose in interest.

"Do you now know me?"

The man was not just handsome; he was breathtaking with his dark tan skin, and Jude had missed that the first time their eyes locked together.

"For I know you, *cairn*." The man smiled wickedly.

Jude knew him, too; he was so familiar, but Jude just couldn't quite place him. Maybe he was someone from his office or a client he had done a presentation for. Jude had definitely seen him somewhere, and the man had to have captured Jude's interest, and so he had filed him away in his subconscious. And no matter what he said now, the towering height, rippling muscles, broad shoulders, wide chest, and long, thickly muscled legs were doing it for him big *time*. Being under the man was something Jude suddenly craved.

"I will have you enter the keep of your own free will, for there can be no mistake that you are claimed and not a prisoner. I will speak to my fenris of your bond."

The man was speaking in circles... his bond? Jude's dreams were getting more convoluted by the second. And what the hell was a fenris?

Leaning over, the man buried his face in Jude's hair and inhaled deeply. "In all my days... your scent, your eyes, your skin... I have never seen another like you. I had thought to stand guard until the end of my days but now... now I will bide with you, for you are my own."

Even though Jude had no idea what his dream man was talking about, it did not stop him from reacting. He was instantly covered in goose bumps from head to toe.

"My name is Eoin…Eoin Thral."

Where had Jude heard that before?

"I want you to say my name, but you cannot as you are now." Eoin exhaled before gently, slowly, removing the gag he had put in place moments before. "Now you will speak it," he ordered, pulling back and looking down at Jude. His eyes locked on the younger man's before he lifted his head and scanned his surroundings. Jude felt the energy leaping off him, like he was excited and tense and scared all at the same time. Just looking at the man, at Eoin, was twisting him up inside.

When Jude said nothing, Eoin's black eyes returned to his.

"Speak my name."

"Eoin," Jude said quickly.

"Good." The big man took a breath. "Now, if you make a sound, I will send you to the dark, *cairn*, I will have no other path to choose."

As Jude did not want to be knocked out, dream or not, he nodded quickly to let the man know that he understood the threat.

"You belong to me, and now will I show you."

There was no mistaking the meaning of those words. Jude barely caught his breath before Eoin's hands were all over him. The blanket was stripped away, and then the coat beneath it was yanked off as well. Jude fought, but Eoin didn't notice; he was so much stronger than the smaller man. But when Eoin tugged off the sweater and then the T-shirt under it, Jude went wild.

"Get off me!" Jude whispered the shout, remembering the threat from earlier, not wanting to be knocked out.

Eoin grabbed both Jude's wrists and held them pinned over his head. With his other hand he started unfastening his belt buckle. Jude twisted under the larger man and got his knee wedged up between them.

"No," Eoin said softly, instantly stilling, the realization like a physical blow that he was scaring Jude. "Fear me not, *cairn*, for I mean you no harm."

The pain in the man's voice froze Jude as Eoin bent his face close. Their breath mingled as he stared down into Jude's eyes. "You are mine, *cairn*, you cannot fight me. I stayed longer than was needed only to be at your side. You make me mad with wanting you. You will not deny me; 'tis not your right."

Jude had no idea what he was talking about but the liquid of his eyes, the heat in them and the way his breath was catching, all of it told Jude that he was wanted desperately. The shiver that ran through Eoin's huge frame was also very telling.

In that moment, Jude understood that if he pushed Eoin away, he would go. The man was being rough with him, demanding, but he would never force himself on him. Eoin was staring into Jude's eyes, willing him to understand, to really see him, to see his intentions and his heart.

"Who are you?" Jude whispered, all fear gone, only interest remaining.

Eoin swallowed hard, releasing Jude's wrists. "I am your mate."

Of course he was. It was a great dream. "Oh yeah, my mate." Jude sucked in his breath, licking his lips.

"Aye." Eoin's voice was broken, a rasping whisper as he leaned slowly toward Jude. "I am your mate as you are mine."

Jude noticed when Eoin stopped moving and just stared at him. He realized then that if he wanted the kiss, he would have to ask for it. And since it was suddenly all he wanted…. "Kiss me," he whispered.

Eoin just stared down into Jude's bottomless brown eyes. Having never kissed anyone in his life, he was unsure of how to proceed. He had bedded many but had never been asked for a kiss.

"Please." Jude's voice was like a caress.

Eoin slid an arm around the younger man's waist and pulled him close, all the time feeling as though his heart was going to beat out of his chest at any moment. When Eoin bent forward, Jude lifted his chin for the kiss.

"I…." Eoin stopped a hairsbreadth from Jude's lips. "I have never—"

Jude reached for him, his fingers sliding up the back of Eoin's neck, pulling the bigger man down so that Jude could claim his mouth.

Eoin Thral had never felt anything like the soft lips pressed to his, the tongue sliding along the seam of his lips, and the gentle nuzzling at the corner of his mouth.

"Open for me," Jude demanded, his voice husky and low as he sucked Eoin's bottom lip between his moist lips.

Eoin was trembling with expectation, loving the feel of Jude nibbling his flesh, his warm breath, the feel of his body pressing against him. The whimper of need rose up out of him as he parted his lips. The idea of such a strong, powerful man held in check by innocence and desire was overwhelming for Jude. The man had never been kissed? Jude would fix that.

Slanting his mouth over Eoin's, Jude's tongue swept inside the man's mouth, exploring him, ravishing him, tasting him, devouring him. There was heat and need and overwhelming gentleness.

Eoin was trembling in Jude's arms, the kiss a revelation. Normally only in the frenzy of rutting did Eoin feel as though his blood was on fire, his body liquid, his heart squeezed in a vise as he released into his partner. But the feelings were only fleeting, lasting for mere moments. Kissing his mate, simply kissing him, burned Eoin up, and the sensations rolled through him, tirelessly, endlessly, unremitting until the man was wild with desire.

"I will make you mine," Eoin roared, breaking the kiss for seconds to take in air before he recaptured Jude's mouth, wanting the delicious sensations to never end.

Eoin's hands made quick work of Jude's belt and the snap and zipper of his jeans. When Jude felt the chill air on his bare skin, he shivered hard. The deep growl in response tore through him, and the kiss was deepened, his mouth stretched wider as Eoin's fingers dug into his back, arms like iron wrapped around him. Jude's head started to pound from lack of air, and just before it hurt, Eoin lifted his lips away, releasing the suction, and flipped Jude over hard on his stomach.

The ground was cold and hard through the thin wool blanket, but only for a second before Jude was lifted to his hands and knees. An arm wound around his hips, anchoring him as a slick hand wrapped around his shaft. Jude realized instantly that he wanted the man just as badly as Eoin wanted him. His brain might have had misgivings, but his body did not. He was hard, almost painfully so. The idea of the big, beautiful man doing things to him was obviously a huge turn-on. And he didn't even need to ask for the man to stop and sheathe himself in latex. No one got diseases from dream men—Jude didn't even have to worry about a condom.

Eoin had no idea about the thoughts that were whirling through Jude's head; he was too consumed with the man's body. The narrow hips and hard stomach, the firm round ass and sensual slope of his back, all the smooth olive skin and his brown curls, never had Eoin seen anything in his life as beautiful as his mate, his heart, his *cairn*.

He cleared his throat to make his voice work. "Inside the keep, in my room, there will be time for me to take you slow but now… there can be only my pleasure as I wish not to go mad."

Jude was shivering under him and not from the cold. When Eoin's hand started to move on his cock, sliding over it, back and forth, squeezing and pulling, he closed his eyes and gave himself up to the needs of his body. It felt so good, the slow stroking, and when he felt a finger slide inside him, he let out a gasp.

"Does this not hurt you, then, *cairn*?" There was genuine surprise there in Eoin's voice.

"No," Jude breathed, his throat dry from his panting. Now he wanted more. Whatever the man was using for lube made the slide smooth and easy. It felt like heaven. "Please."

"You… you would have me…." It sounded like a question.

"Oh hell, yeah, I'm gonna have you," Jude swore.

The promise in Jude's voice made Eoin's heart hurt, and looking at him, touching him…. Eoin could barely breathe as he spread Jude's ass cheeks and pushed gently at his entrance with the head of his cock.

Jude didn't allow even a moment more of hesitation. He pushed back and impaled himself on the long, hard, hot length of Eoin Thral. He was huge and filled Jude like he'd never been before, stretching him, and the pain was sharp and burning for the second before it became piercing, almost overwhelming pleasure.

"Jude…." The strangled groan rasped from Eoin's throat. His hands were on Jude's hips, his fingers digging into his flesh. "I should die here and now, buried inside my *cairn*… my mate… my love."

His love? Cairn *meant love?*

"I meant not to pass through the veil; I never believed in such as a heart for a guardian… how could there be one to want us… savages as we are."

The words made no sense, but the words hardly mattered. Only the man mattered.

"But when I saw you… saw your face, your eyes… that you were a man; then I knew well my path. None of the women who had me ever wanted… they could not take… but you…." Eoin trailed off, his fingers working over Jude's cock as he eased slowly out of his ass. "You have all of me, and your body begs for more."

Eoin punctuated his statement by plowing back inside of him deep and hard, buried again to the hilt before repeating his motion, faster and faster, over and over, pounding in and out of him, all the time his hand keeping the same rhythm on Jude's now-dripping shaft. He kissed and licked and nibbled up Jude's shoulder to the side of his neck, which sent waves of heat dancing over Jude's skin. Eoin Thral was both demanding and physical, and Jude had never known how much he craved being dominated, how much he ached to submit, or that once he'd found out, how consuming his response would be. He was shaking so hard, his entire body throbbing with desire, that when the orgasm ambushed him, stealing his breath, he was allowed only one last ragged moan.

"Your body holds me so tight, *cairn*… and you burn inside… willingly I give you all that I am, if only you will keep me," Eoin begged.

Jude's muscles tightened all at once, clamping down on Eoin's shaft as he lost himself to the throes of his release, the rapture sweeping him away in a wave of euphoria. Arms were suddenly wrapped around him tight as Eoin pushed in so deep the younger man was certain he felt him in his abdomen. The warmth filled him, thickly coating his insides before escaping his body and trickling down his thighs.

"You will be the death of me," Eoin whispered.

Jude's arms were barely holding him up; his muscles had all tensed, and the spasms in his ass were making his whole body tremble. That Eoin was still buried inside him, that he didn't seem to want to move, was a revelation. Dream or not, Jude had learned something about himself. He needed a man like this in real life. He wanted to be dominated and made to submit, all the time knowing that he was loved and treasured and utterly safe.

"Do you feel me inside you, *cairn*?"

Jude nodded.

"There will only ever be me, from now until the end of your days. Those men you call friends will not have you, and you will look for no other but me. Wonder not how you will find another to slake your thirst or feed your hunger, for there will only ever be me."

Jude looked over his shoulder at Eoin, and Eoin pulled out fast, making Jude suck in his breath at the release of the suction and the loss of the feeling of fullness. Eoin's eyes as they raked over him were narrowed in half, the gleam there one of absolute possession. Jude could only imagine what he looked like with cum dripping from his ass, running down the inside of his legs, hair tousled, red marks soon to bruise covering his neck and shoulders.

"You have been ravaged, *cairn*, and well it looks on you."

Jude had to smile. His lover looked so smug, so pleased with himself. He saw delight reflected in the glint in the dark eyes, in the sly curve of his lips, and in the deep sigh that rose out of him.

"You so pleased me," he rasped, and Jude was stunned by the emotion he heard in Eoin's voice.

He was even more surprised when Eoin lunged forward and grabbed him, yanking him into his arms before crushing him to his big hard body, tucking his head under his chin. He could feel Eoin's heart beating against his cheek.

"You will stay at my side until I am done of my days."

He wanted Jude with him until he died? His dream man was very possessive, and Jude loved it. No one had ever wanted to keep Jude. Even Tiernan, who he had been with longer than anyone else, had ended up cheating on him, which basically answered any questions Jude had about forever. Leave it to Jude's overly romantic brain to conjure up a man who was absolutely perfect for him only to have him fade away when he woke up in the morning or came to in the hospital. Jude still wasn't sure where he was going to be when he opened his eyes. If he opened his eyes, maybe he was in a coma?

"Look here to me."

Jude lifted his head, and Eoin bent and kissed him.

The kiss was different from the first time, lingering and slow. Eoin explored Jude's mouth, missing nothing, stroking his tongue with Jude's, breathing him in. One long, languid kiss led to another and another, each deeper, more erotic, more claiming than the last, letting Jude know that he could kiss him for as long as he wanted. He belonged to Eoin. When Eoin finally eased back, Jude leaned with him, trying to keep contact with his new, demanding lover.

The deep chuckle brought Jude's attention to his face.

"You smell like me, *cairn*, and while I am loathe to change this, I feel you must bathe."

"Bathe?"

The smile was evil, the look in his eyes smoldering. "Fret not, love."

When Eoin stood up, Jude's eyes followed him. The man was tall and strong, covered in rippling muscles and deeply tanned brown skin. His whole body was toned and hard, and Jude knew from being in his arms that his skin was hot to the touch. He needed to be back under him, tangled with him, and when Jude voiced his desire, Eoin's eyes glowed hot and molten.

"I knew I would be in your blood the moment I took you, *cairn*."

"How?" Jude asked him, his eyes sliding down to the uncut cock and the heavy balls that nestled it. Even at rest the shaft was huge, and the thought that it had been inside him, filling him, was almost too much for Jude to bear. He felt his face flood with heat. Jude had never before found foreskin appealing, the look so different from his own, but with Eoin, it was natural, primal, and sexy as hell. Everything about the man appealed to him; there was nothing that didn't make his mouth water.

"I know you, love," Eoin answered.

"Of course you do." Jude took a nervous breath, smiling up at the man, a deep sigh following. "It's my dream after all."

One eyebrow arched rakishly before there was like a pulse in the air, a gentle push against Jude's entire body, before he was faced with his dog, Joe.

"Oh shit!" Jude yelped, leaping to his feet, scrambling backward, hitting a tree so hard that he gasped. Joe moved fast, reaching him and sitting at his feet, looking up at Jude, head tipped to the side the way dogs do when they're not sure what's going on with you. "Holy shit," Jude breathed, finally getting in the air he needed to make sound.

There was the pulse again, and Jude felt it like a wave of power sliding over his skin before he was again faced with a man.

"'Tis how I know you, and your scent that drives me mad, and your warm smooth skin...." Eoin trailed off, falling to his knees in front of Jude. "I will taste you now as I have wanted to since the moment I first opened my eyes and saw yours."

The second Eoin's hands were on him Jude got hard. And when Eoin took him inside his hot, wet mouth, Jude lengthened and grew, much to the man's pleasure. Even without benefit of technique, just hard, rough sucking, Jude felt his toes curl in response. There was no finesse, it was not the blow job Jude could give. It was primitive and passionate, the suction fierce as Eoin took Jude down his throat. The action spoke to Eoin's need, and what he needed more than anything was Jude.

"Eoin...." He rasped out the man's name as he felt the demanding tongue slide over the tip of his cock, along the hard shaft and back. The swirling, tugging motion was slowly driving Jude out of his mind. The throbbing pressure was filling his body with white hot, blinding, building heat.

He buried his hands in Eoin's hair trying to move him off him before he came, but the quick shake of his head let Jude know that this was what his lover wanted: to drink him down. Jude felt weightless as he rocked into Eoin's mouth, like he had exploded and there were only fragments of him left, millions of pieces raining down over Eoin.

Jude shuddered under his hands, watched the cording muscles in Eoin's neck as the man swallowed, and then watched his tongue lick him clean. It was the sexiest thing Jude had ever seen in his life, and when Eoin rose, Jude reached for the man's now semi-erect cock.

"No," Eoin said quickly, spinning him around, shoving him against the tree. "Grab hold."

The bark of the tree was frozen and hard, but Jude held tight as he felt a finger slide over his crease and then quickly inside.

"What is that?" Jude asked softly, catching his breath, caring only that the fingers were slick, only absently wondering what the lubrication was that made it so.

"Cooking oil," Eoin answered in Jude's ear before he brushed a finger over his prostate and his world exploded in bliss. Eoin's breath was warm before he bit down on Jude's shoulder. "I will learn ways to make you wet but had not the time."

Never had Jude had such a voracious partner; if the man did any more to him, he was sure his heart would explode.

"Let me suck you," Jude pleaded even as he felt the head of Eoin's cock slip between his cheeks, spreading them, easing closer to his already puckering hole.

"There will be time," Eoin growled, and Jude felt the deep rumble in his chest against his back. "For now I cannot think of any but being inside you once more."

Jude couldn't breathe.

"My name is Eoin Thral, and you, Jude Shea, belong to me," he said before he plunged deep into him with one powerful forward thrust.

Jude gasped, and Eoin pulled out a little only to bury himself in deeper, harder, faster, sliding in and out while he held Jude's hips and kept him still, pinned to the tree, with his teeth on the back of his neck.

"Mine," Eoin growled savagely, lifting Jude up off his feet as he hit his gland with every stroke, making it impossible for Jude not to scream. Eoin's total control, his absolute dominance, and the hand that slid over his mouth, muffling the sound, made it all even hotter. When Jude came, his orgasm blinding and consuming, he surrendered himself to his lover, melting into the embrace, the furnace of Eoin's body, and the depths of his eyes.

Eoin watched the man trembling under him, took in the long line of his throat as his head was thrown back, the curve of his bowed spine, the lean muscles covering the sinewy frame, and the perfect ass that he was buried in. Never in his life had he seen anything more alluring than his mate. As Eoin's hand slid down over the flat, cut stomach, he pressed hard, feeling the muscles clenching under his palm. The strength in the man was nearly as alluring as his beauty. When Jude turned to look over his shoulder at Eoin, the guardian's heart stopped. To see Jude's eyes clouded with passion, heavy-lidded, looking like he was drunk, to hear his sharp indrawn breath and feel his tight channel squeezing him so tight, it was more than Eoin could have ever dreamed of. His life that was filled with peril and pain had just been blessed. Whatever it took, whatever sacrifices needed to be made, he would willingly make to keep the man in his arms with him.

"Eoin," Jude breathed out his name.

There was an explosion behind his eyes as he plunged down into Jude, so deep, so hard, filling him with liquid heat, feeling as though his very soul was running out of him and into his lover.

"I don't wanna wake up." Jude smiled at him.

"You are my own, Jude Shea, only my own." Eoin inhaled his mate's delicious scent deeply before he twisted Jude's head so he could grind his mouth down against Jude's lips.

And because it was a statement of absolute fact, Jude was suddenly certain that he really was wide awake in the middle of the woods. After he pushed Eoin back to stare up into his eyes, his new lover laughed at the stunned expression on Jude's face.

"Aye, *cairn*." The velvet sound of his voice resonated inside Jude. "Truly, you dream not."

None of it was a dream: not the man, the fall, none of it. Jude was awake, and everything was real. It made sense that the ground rose up to grab him as he passed out cold.

Chapter Six

IT WAS a blur. The path through the forest became a muddy track that turned into a narrow dirt road and then a wide one. Where there had been only the trees and the moonlight there were now other people, scattered travelers forced out into the night by necessity. Jude's mind was racing, and every time he felt like he had a second of clarity, a toehold in reality, it would be instantly pulled away by the man at his side.

Riding, a horse no less, Jude had never been in the saddle in his life and was now expected to endure it after his ass had taken its own pounding. He was uncomfortable and sore, and he wanted answers.

Eoin would not talk to him; he was more concerned with the entrance they would make together. Apparently, Jude dressed as he was, riding his own horse, was of paramount importance.

When Jude revived from his shock, he had a second to get his bearings before Eoin tossed him into an icy stream to clean the sweat, semen, and oil from his body. The soap was something Jude had not encountered before: coarse, more a cake of seeds than anything else. It smelled like pine, but it was abrasive against his skin. So between the glacier-cold water, having his skin scrubbed off, and being generally exhausted, his mood had gone from a post-coital euphoria to irritated and prickly.

Jude's clothes were not suitable either. After the drowning—or bath as Eoin called it—Jude was dressed in long underwear that laced up his crotch, soft brown leather pants, a long-sleeved white linen shirt, and boots that came up to his knees. He was a cross between a Native American Indian and a pirate. The only concession Eoin had made was Jude's T-shirt. He got to put that back on because otherwise the shirt was too scratchy to wear. Feeling waterlogged and chilled to the bone, Jude wanted his pea coat but was instead covered by a heavy, quilted jacket and then another sleeveless piece that had a high collar in the back of his neck. The clothes fit, but not well; they had obviously belonged to someone else. But when Jude asked Eoin who their owner was, he didn't or wouldn't say.

"Did they belong to your lover?" Jude asked softly when Eoin turned to step away from him.

Eoin turned back fast and fisted his hand in Jude's hair as he yanked Jude's head back, his lips hovering over his lover's. "I have taken women to my bed, but never have I had another who wanted me as I want them and would give themselves to me freely… until you."

Jude nodded, and Eoin bent and kissed him deeply, slowly, savoring his taste and the uninhibited way Jude kissed him back, their tongues tangling. When Jude lifted his arms, wrapped them around his neck, and nearly climbed Eoin's body to keep their lips sealed together, Eoin chuckled into his mouth. His heart swelled just knowing that Jude wanted him, and when he lifted the smaller man into his arms, patting his tight little ass, and felt Jude's long, muscular legs as they wrapped around his waist, a wave of contentment washed over him.

Jude's body fit Eoin's like a glove; his carnal appetite matched Eoin's; the flicker of jealousy he had heard in Jude's voice when he thought there had been another man in Eoin's bed let him know Jude was already possessive of him. Jude wanted to belong to him, and that filled Eoin with a calm that he had never felt before. Even in the face of Jude's darkening mood, Eoin's feelings of rapture did not diminish. He liked listening to the man complain about his backside, because he knew *he* was responsible for the ache in it.

Jude was unaware of his lover's attention because he was nodding off and trying to stay on the horse at the same time. When he heard a sharp whistle, he tensed and straightened in his saddle, nearly upsetting his already precarious balance.

"I will speak for you, *cairn*," Eoin said under his breath as four men rode quickly toward them.

From his tone, Jude was sure the topic was not up for debate. And that was fine with him; he didn't want to talk to the Vikings anyway.

They were four of the biggest men Jude had ever seen in his life, all dressed similarly to Eoin; the same leather pants tucked into knee-high leather boots and heavy quilted shirts, but no coats, even though it was freezing and the wind was whistling around them. They were all carrying weapons on their saddles as well, a long sword on one side, a halberd on the other, and a dagger at their belt. It was like being at a Renaissance Fair. Jude dropped his head so he wouldn't smile.

"Fear them not, *cairn*," Eoin said quickly, thinking that the armament had frightened his mate, wanting to put his mind at ease.

Jude lifted his head and shot Eoin a look. Jude should have been scared; he knew that, but it just reminded him so much of the *larping*—live-action role-playing—that his older brother used to do that it was really hard to keep a straight face. *Dungeons & Dragons* had been big at the Shea home.

"Are you not—"

"I'm fine," Jude assured the big man, his smile causing Eoin's chest to tighten.

The men greeted Eoin excitedly, warmly, thrilled that he was back as they had all feared for his life when he had been set upon by outlanders and disappeared. Eoin explained, while Jude listened, that he had not been chased by outlanders, but by gryphons.

"How could this be?" one man asked, his attention divided between Eoin and Jude. "Why would gryphons attack you? They report only to the king."

It was interesting to Jude that the others didn't have Eoin's same speech pattern or dialect. They sounded colder to him. Harder. He preferred the warmth and resonance of Eoin's voice, the way the words came out, especially when he was overwhelmed with powerful emotion.

"Aye," Eoin said softly, "and with my own eyes did I see Cuyler Adon."

"Why would the captain of the king's royal guard be hunting a guardian of Drelindah Holt?"

"Have the words of the baroness finally angered him?" another asked. "Do you believe the king will turn the wrath he has shown others to Saraso and—"

Another man spoke up. "We will speak inside with the baroness," The way everyone deferred to him, Jude understood that he was the man in charge. The man tipped his head at Jude. "Who rides with the guardian?"

"There is much to say," Eoin said solemnly, "but I was forced through the veil."

Jude heard the breath squeezed from every man's chest, saw the looks of horror and amazement at the same time, felt the nervous anticipation flowing off them. Time stood still.

"I have found my *cairn*."

Jude expected a different reaction. Eoin had told him that before him, there had only been women so Jude had expected them to be less than thrilled to hear that Eoin was suddenly gay. But their faces showed only wonder and interest and something Jude could not read. Had he known that the mate of a guardian was simply accepted, their sex meaningless and only the bond of any importance, he would not have been so amazed at the lack of shock on the faces of Eoin's fellow guardians.

Eoin watched the way the other guardians eyed his mate and found it unsettling. The interest in Jude that Eoin's fenris, Drist Circ, the man's whose word Eoin lived and died by, especially unnerved him.

"Come inside," Drist said absently to Eoin, his eyes sliding over Jude Shea, taking in the tousled curls, dark eyes, and swollen lips. "There is much to say."

As they all rode toward the enormous structure, huge wooden gates opened, and Jude marveled at how large the area was inside. There were cottages everywhere, and then at the top of a hill what looked like a small castle, if *small* and *castle* could be used in the same sentence. He felt like he had been dropped into every medieval movie he had ever seen. There were guards walking along the walls, and Jude saw that some carried longbows, others crossbows, and all had swords hanging from scabbards at their sides. It was so weird, so surreal, and Jude had to shake his head to make sure he was still awake.

They dismounted in front of the keep, and several boys came and took the horses away after Eoin removed the saddlebags. Eoin kept Jude at his side, his hand firmly on the back of his neck as he guided him up the stone stairs. At the top, Drist pushed against the enormous iron-belted door, and it swung slowly open to reveal the warmth and rich aroma of the Baroness of Saraso's home. Five steps led down into the main hall of the keep, and Jude looked up at the vaulted ceiling several feet above them. Brightly colored pennants hung from the wooden beams, and there were armor and shields on every wall. There were several large tapestries depicting battles and a shrine in one corner.

"Cleanse your hands," Eoin directed Jude, gesturing toward the small basin near the door. It was built into the wall, and a small cloth hung in a steel ring above it.

Jude washed his hands first, and then Eoin and the others followed.

"This is the home of our baroness," Drist told Jude, gesturing around the room. "She will join us here at once."

"Fear not," Eoin told Jude, his hand settling on his shoulder. "I am here."

When Jude turned to him, looked up at him with his big brown eyes, Eoin noticed instantly how warm they were, how soft, the lashes framing them so long and black, fragile, like the rest of the man. Eoin wondered how Jude was not aware of how captivating he was.

"Eoin!"

Everyone turned at once as a woman flew across the room toward them. Since all the rest of the men sank down to the floor on one knee, Jude did the same.

"No, no, no," she cried, and Eoin, understanding, stood at the same second she flung herself at him. Arms were wrapped around his neck as she buried her face in his shoulder and sobbed.

Jude liked her immediately; the baroness had been worried, and that warmed his heart.

"I was told that outlanders were hunting you, and I was ready to send Arius up the mountain to speak to Crispin Ebudai and find out the meaning of—"

"They were not outlanders, lady," Eoin said, putting her down gently on her feet. "They were gryphons. 'Twas Cuyler Adon wanting you to believe that I was killed by outlanders."

Her scowl was instant. "Cuyler Adon is captain of the king's royal guard."

"Aye," Eoin agreed.

"I do not…." Her words trailed off as she looked around at the men crowded close to her. "I did not believe Crispin Ebudai when he told me at our last parlay that I had to be watchful of the king now that I had signed a treaty with him. I never thought my own monarch would fear me enough to try and kill me."

No one said a word as they let hers sink in.

"The king thinks to take my guardians first. He will kill the men who protect me, and when I am vulnerable, he will strike and blame the outlanders for whatever atrocity he has his gryphons commit on my land and my people." She took a shuddering breath. "The king will use my death and the destruction of my holding to call for war with the outlanders."

"He will surge up the mountain and kill every man, woman, and child that he finds," Greshan Kai, her domo, the man in charge of her home, said solemnly.

"The king wants your holding," Drist told her. "It is the richest in all of Midrin. If he has Saraso as well as the pass, he has the outlanders and all their land and resources as well."

"They will not be easy to conquer," Greshan assured the others. "The outlanders are strong and brave and know the terrain as the king's men do not."

"Such an action will last a lifetime," Drelindah breathed, "and is just what the king needs to refill the treasury. Nothing fills coffers like war."

There was another long silence.

"But Eoin has thankfully survived," Greshan said hopefully, "so that we may prepare for the attack and the coming of the king."

"We must prepare ourselves for war." Drist said with absolute conviction.

"Aye, but first must we send new messengers to Crispin Ebudai," Eoin told the baroness. "We need his help, and without Saraso guarding the Ellandrel pass, his home will be overrun by royal troops, he needs to send men to aid us."

"Aye," Drelindah agreed. "You and Drist and Arius shall ascend the mountain to parlay with the man. We need his men fighting alongside ours."

"Crispin Ebudai will not believe the likes of me, lady," Eoin told her.

"He will, Eoin, you are my guardian." All eyes were on her. "We must make haste or all our kith and kin will be slaughtered along with all others who are caught in the king's murderous web."

In the silence that descended, Drelindah Holt, Baroness of Saraso, finally noticed Jude Shea for the first time. "But who is this that I have so freely spoken my mind in front of?" the baroness asked suddenly, wary as she stepped out of the circle of men to face Jude.

He started to drop back down to one knee, but she stopped him with a hand on his arm. When his eyes met hers, she gasped.

"Brown," she said breathlessly. "I have never seen such a color."

Brown? She'd never seen brown eyes before? Was she kidding? "Everybody has brown eyes," he said as he smiled at her.

"Not on *this* side of the veil," she told him, her eyes gliding over his face, seeing the chiseled features and smooth, flawless skin. "Nor do we have men so delicate and fair. Tell me... to whom do you belong, veiler?"

There was only one answer to give. "I belong to Eoin Thral."

She whirled around to face her guardian, her heart in her throat. She was both exhilarated and crushed at the very same time. "Eoin Thral... you have found your *cairn*?"

He answered, holding no false illusions that he was loved, but a guardian was a rare commodity, and after he spoke, she would have five instead of six. That she was losing one of the men who protected her—that thought would vex her. "Aye, Baroness, he is my heart."

She sucked in her breath as the overwhelming happiness slammed through her. When she turned back to face Jude, he noticed that her eyes were sparkling with tears. "My guardian has traveled through the veil and found his mate... by the five gods of Astyn, I am well pleased."

Jude smiled back at her, and Eoin, watching both his mate and his baroness, could not speak. He had never imagined she truly cared for him, but he saw now that he had been completely wrong.

The woman, his baroness, cared about him and his happiness.

"But sadly, a mate of a guardian is no more welcome in my plotting than a wife of a soldier." She sighed heavily. "And he has no place here with my guardians and retainers. You must retire to Eoin's room and await him there, for we will speak on until near rise."

Jude was at a loss.

The baroness clapped her hands, and a woman appeared at a doorway to the right. "Show the *cairn* of my guardian to his room. Wake the others; I need a meal prepared now."

"Aye, baroness," the woman agreed quickly, motioning for Jude to come to her.

Jude looked up to see if that was what Eoin wanted him to do, but he was already being led from the room. Her word being law, when the baroness waved a dismissive hand at him, he moved fast, bolting across the room to reach the serving woman.

On the curving stairs, Jude was silent, just following the woman carrying the candle lantern. She explained that Eoin's room was at the end of a long stone hallway and that she would see to the fire, as it was too cold a night to go without one. Jude agreed with her the second she opened the door. Inside it was like an icy, dark cell. He hated it instantly.

An hour later, with the fire blazing away in the small hearth and the room finally beginning to warm, Jude started to feel better and hated the room a little less. Never again would he think his one-bedroom apartment was small. Eoin's room was the definition of small. There was a fireplace, a window that wasn't designed to open, a small bed, a table, two chairs, and bucket for relieving yourself. There was a small linen towel draped over the top of it. There was no toilet paper because there wasn't a toilet. There was a large bowl to wash your face in and a huge pitcher of freezing water sitting beside it on the table. It was hell, and Jude was starving.

He realized that he had skipped lunch that day only to come home and find Cuyler on his doorstep trying to steal his dog. And now he knew that Joe was really Eoin and was, in fact, not a dog, but a guardian. Cuyler Adon was a gryphon, whatever that was. And Jude was stuck in a time he didn't know and a place he didn't know without his cell phone or his laptop. It was just *bad*.

The knock on the door startled him. In his T-shirt, pants, and boots he answered the door. The woman there looked like she had been awakened from a dead sleep.

Jude spoke gently. "Hello?"

Her brows furrowed, and she looked at him and then above him at the door and then back to him. "You are not Eoin Thral."

Obviously not. "No."

She yawned loudly. "I am Kennis, and sent I was by Justine to warm the bed of the guardian."

He squinted at her, feeling his stomach clench and a flush of heat. Realization came fast: he was mad, *really mad,* but why the hell for? It was an innocent mistake, so why did just the thought of Eoin in bed with someone else make his blood boil? "Well, Justine, whoever that is, was mistaken; I'm the only one sleeping with Eoin Thral. I'm his mate—*cairn*, whatever… I'm *it*, so don't worry about warming anything. Thanks but no thanks."

She stared at him.

He stared back. Why had he sounded so surly when he finished? How could he be jealous? He barely knew the man!

Her eyes widened, and the smile followed. "Truly, Eoin has a *cairn*?"

Now Jude was confused. "Yes."

"Oh!" she squealed. "Gods be praised! I will tell the other girls straight away!"

And with that she was gone, whirling around and disappearing down the hall into the darkness.

"This place is so weird," Jude muttered, closing and bolting the door. She had seemed happy, thrilled even, and he didn't get that at all. A half hour later there was a new knock on his door, and when he answered it, there were five girls on the other side: Kennis, one with fruit, and another with bread, another with some kind of dried fish that smelled nasty, and the last with something that smelled like wine.

He smiled at them all. "Hi."

"May we enter?" Kennis asked him, smiling back, looking as though she had brushed her hair and added some ribbons to the tangled mass.

"Sure," Jude said, opening the door and letting them all in.

It was like a slumber party. They all wanted to talk to him and look at him and more than anything, touch his hair and his skin and wonder at the color of his eyes. Brown was enchanting for them, and when Jude explained that most everyone he knew back home had brown eyes, they were simply astounded. The only thing more amazing was his soft-as-butter T-shirt, which they all took turns smoothing their hands over. Soon it was apparent, even to Jude, that the T-shirt was not the draw; but his six-pack abs underneath were. He let them all stroke their hands over his abdomen and through his hair and down the curve of his back. It was harmless, and the way they all twittered over him reminded him of happy hour on Friday night at home.

The wine was cherry, and it was good, but he soon realized that it had a little more kick to it than the regular red wine he was used to drinking. It was good; he drank a ton of it, and then asked a lot of questions about guardians that all the women were more than happy to answer.

Guardians lived with a baron or baroness and were their private guards. Normally there were two or four, but depending on the wealth of the barony there could be more. The baroness of Saraso had six guardians, of which Eoin Thral was one. Guardians were fed and sheltered like the rest of the men, but the difference was that they were quartered in the keep with the baron or baroness, as they were expected to be on guard day and night.

As guardians were considered more beasts than men, most women steered clear of them. There might be one every so often whose curiosity got the better of her, but one night with a guardian usually cured any prolonged interest. They were savage beasts, dogs first and men second, but still they had the same appetites, and so a baron or baroness was forced to house between five and ten women on their land whose specific duty was to sleep with the guardians. To bed a guardian was painful and rough, and many felt that it was rape, even though they had given their consent. All the kept women dreaded being called to the room of a guardian.

"Why do it, then?" Jude asked Kennis. "Why don't you do something else?"

"I have an easy life." She smiled at him. "I lie on my back perhaps three nights in seven, and for the rest I am left to my own to do as I like. I am fed, clothed, and paid a small stipend that I may take with me when I finally leave. Why would I do any other than this?"

"But what about falling in love, getting married, or having children?"

"We may all of us do as you say once we leave the barony."

Jude didn't understand her thinking, and neither did he understand when Kennis told him that of all the guardians, Eoin

Thral was the one who they all hated servicing the most.

"The others will beat you or scratch and tear your skin. Orim will take you until you can no longer stand, Drist will lash you to his bed… but Eoin just takes you as one dog does another, but with his hand on your throat, and he never speaks," Kennis told him. "I often believed that one night he would simply snap me in half, and that would be the end of my days."

All the women took turns nodding in agreement.

Jude was amazed. How could these women think that the man he knew could ever hurt them?

"Come, Jude," Kennis said as a few of the other women started trickling out. "Let me ride you; I burn even now."

He rolled over on his stomach and reached for her hand, turning it over to kiss her palm. "What would the guardian say?"

Apparently that question held weight because he saw her shudder with fear.

He smiled lazily up at her. "How 'bout a kiss."

Never had Kennis seen a more beautiful man. She wanted to ravish his mouth, but he would allow only a chaste peck.

The other girls took turns kissing him good-night and followed Kennis from the room. Jude rose with some difficulty, stumbled to the door, and locked it behind them, but then thought better of it, unsure if he fell asleep how Eoin would get in. In bed, it was warm suddenly, almost hot, and so he stripped off his clothes before he closed his eyes.

EOIN was going out of his mind. He had been led from the room by his fenris and had been unable to even gift his mate with a smile when he took his leave of him. Sequestered for hours, Eoin had no choice but to drive Jude from his thoughts while he dealt with pressing matters of war. His loyalty to his mistress, to the barony, knew no bounds but was suddenly hampered with concern for Jude. He could not be reckless anymore; his life was no longer his own. It belonged to Jude. And what must his mate be thinking after long hours left abandoned in a strange place? That Eoin cared nothing for him?

Finally free to go to his room, all the plotting and conspiring finished for the evening, Eoin hurried to reach his mate. He needed to see Jude, to talk to him, to touch him and make sure he was safe. All his life he had lived in the holding at Saraso, and never had there been even a flicker of concern for his own safety. But suddenly, nowhere in his world seemed a secure enough site for Jude. His mate was safest in his own world, in Chicago, and that was where Eoin would take him as soon as he was able. Jogging now, he realized that he would feel so much better as soon as he could lay eyes on his mate… and hands. Yes, hands would be even better than eyes.

As Eoin made his way down the hall to his room, the words of his mistress haunted him.

"When will you take your *cairn* and leave my home, Eoin Thral?"

There was no question that he would leave, only her question of when. For a guardian who had found his mate, his heart, could no longer serve as protector. Without their mates, guardians were stoic and cold, with no other thought or concern but the protection of their masters. Once they found their mates, which only one in a hundred ever did, the place of the master was taken by the place of the mate, their *cairn*. If and when a guardian found their heart, they were released from their service at once. In Eoin's case, never again could his life be solely dedicated to the protection of Drelindah Holt, because now everything that he was belonged to Jude.

Eoin Thral was no longer shackled to the life of solitude and service, instead he was now able to have his own home, his own life. Even as Drelindah was genuinely thrilled for Eoin Thral, she would miss knowing he was there protecting her. He made her feel utterly safe and invulnerable, and once he left so would the comfort of his presence.

The door to Eoin's room was closed but not locked. Jude had probably thought it was secured, not knowing that the bar had to be both lifted and slid into place. Eoin made a mental note to show his mate how to make the room safe against late-night intruders.

"Eoin." He heard the soft call as he opened the door and saw Jude draped over his bed, the blankets pulled only far enough to cover the curve of the firm ass. He groaned as he turned to look at Drist.

"Aye, my fenris?"

Drist walked up in front of Eoin and put his hand on the door, pushing it open a little more so he too could see into the room. "Your man is fetching and fey," he began, and Eoin felt his stomach begin to knot. Drist continued. "I claim my right as your fenris and will lay with him. Find my bed; one of the maids is there."

The words so casually spoken made Eoin's heart hurt. His stomach twisted and lurched, and bile rose in his throat. Never had he had anything worth having, worth wanting, worth taking—until now. Now there was Jude, the only perfection in his life, the only piece that was his alone, and now his fenris, the man who would decide his future, the man who along with Drelindah's father Ashron Holt had trained him and raised him, now he wanted Eoin's mate. The shock twisted fast into a simmering rage. The man dared to think of taking Eoin's place.

"Hey."

Eoin turned to look into the room and saw that Jude had rolled over on his back, revealing his beautiful semi-erect cock and looking at him with those dark, deep heavy-lidded eyes.

"Come here."

He swallowed hard, and Drist pushed the door open, revealing that he was there as well.

"Oh." Jude giggled, still tipsy from drinking earlier, and moved fast, sitting, pulling his knees up, and bringing the blanket with him so he was now covered to his stomach. "Sorry. Didn't see ya. You guys all done with the whole talking about stuff that mates and wives can't be a part of?"

"Aye," Drist said, taking a step into the room, looking at Eoin and dismissing him with a tip of his head. "We need to find our beds."

"Good." Jude smiled, looking past him at Eoin. "I missed you. I never knew what it felt like to be married… I mean, mated."

Married… mated. The words swam in Eoin's brain for moments before he caught his breath. Slipping around Drist, he went to stand beside his bed and his mate. "Aye, you are mated, and no married or mated women… or man… may be taken on Drelindah Holt's land. It is her mandate. Her law."

Each baron or baroness had laws for the people who lived under their protection; one of Drelindah's being to protect all vows made on her land. Between married people, those engaged or mated, she saw no difference. If you were bound to another by word or by benefit of clergy, the union was inviolate. No one could be claimed or taken who already belonged to another.

"Yeah, I heard all about guardians tonight." Jude smiled up at Eoin and found that he was looking at Drist instead of him. "Hey."

The big man returned his gaze to his mate, only to find Jude's eyes catching the light from the fire, looking like dark smoky topaz. He could barely breathe.

"You guys are considered scary, huh?" Jude teased him.

"We are," Eoin managed to get out, his voice a hoarse rasp.

"You don't scare me, guardian," Jude said softly. "I'm your mate."

It took a minute for Eoin to tear his gaze from Jude's and look at Drist. "Fenris," he called to him. "Heard you his words?"

"Aye," Drist grunted, his groin hardening almost painfully at the sight of the beautiful, sleepy-eyed man in the other guardian's bed. He could smell his skin, knew it would be warm under his hands, knew the lips on his would be soft and wet, and knew too that Eoin Thral had no intention of sharing his mate now or ever. And truthfully, Drist knew, neither would he, had he ever found his own _cairn_. Having never been blessed, Drist had lived his life as a guardian only for the baroness. Eoin's life now belonged to Jude, and the older man was sick with jealousy. "I heard your words," he said, nodding slowly, his eyes locked on Eoin's, "and know their meaning."

Eoin nodded, and Drist saw the steely resolve in the younger man.

"We leave at rise," Drist mumbled before he turned and quickly left the room.

Eoin moved to the door and bolted it securely shut, making certain that it could not be opened. He then turned to look at his mate.

"We have a lot to talk about," Jude assured him.

But Eoin couldn't speak. He could barely breathe. Whether

Jude knew it or not, he had armed Eoin with what he needed to drive Drist away. Eoin did not want to fight with his mentor but had seen no other choice. He would not, could not, allow another man to lie with his mate, and so had been preparing to attack Drist when Jude had saved him. He was so thankful, so overcome, that when Jude lifted his arms to him, Eoin leaned down and grabbed the smaller man, crushing him to his heart, burying his face in the soft, silky curls.

"What's wrong? You're shaking?"

The concern for him, the way the embrace tightened, and the long sigh made Eoin tremble hard, his vision blurring, the muscles in his jaw clenching. "Loathe was I to leave your side, love."

Jude felt the hands sliding down his back, and he moved forward until he was on his knees in front of him. Eoin pulled him the rest of the way into his lap, and Jude's legs wrapped around his back. With his straining cock pushing up against Jude's crease through his lambskin breeches and Jude's hard, leaking shaft pressing against his stomach, leaving wet spots on his shirt front, Eoin knew the man in his arms was just as aroused as he was. And even though the physical manifestation of their love was good, amazing, soul-consuming ecstasy, it was the love that pushed it over into a mating, a joining of not just flesh, but souls as well. It was the love for his mate that set Eoin on fire, engulfed him, strengthened, and nourished him. All he needed was Jude, because he loved him already, that quickly, in a matter of days. He had fallen so hard that his heart hurt almost constantly. Only the words would ease the ache inside, only the forever words would soothe him. He needed Jude to tell him he loved him and would stay with him, wherever, forever, until the day he died.

Eoin rubbed his chin over the top of Jude's hair and clutched him tight, kissing his forehead, letting his fingers trace his spine as Jude shifted in his lap, pushing down, sliding back and forth over the ridge in Eoin's pants.

"Jude, I have no... there is no oil to... I would hurt you."

"Then make sure you don't," Jude said, the wine, the heat of the room, and the gorgeous sexy man holding him in his arms, everything combining to make his body hard and throbbing. "Fuck me."

It took Eoin a moment to be able to speak. "What is... *fucking?*"

"You balls-deep in my ass... that's fucking."

Eoin's body went up in flames. *Fucking*, what a filthy and delicious-sounding word.

"Come on," Jude said, wriggling out of Eoin's arms so he could go to his hands and knees on the bed. "I wanna talk to you, but I can't even think until you fuck my brains out, so just do it already, 'cause I really wanna talk to you."

Eoin wanted to talk to him and *fuck* him and sleep beside him. It was too much to dream and unbelievable to feel. As Jude leaned face down on the bed, lifting his ass higher into the air, Eoin was sure he was going to erupt right there without even making it inside the man. Instead, he leaned forward as he fumbled with his clothes and buried his tongue deep in his mate's ass.

Jude nearly came off the bed. The catch of breath made Eoin's balls draw up tight, almost painfully as he concentrated on pushing his tongue through the tight ring of muscle in Jude's hole, swirling wide, slippery strokes, moving deeper with every thrust, making everything wet and slick with saliva. He sucked and licked until Jude screamed his name, begging him, pumping his own cock with the pre-come dripping from it.

Watching his mate, seeing him writhe and buck, hearing him moan, pant, and whimper, it was too much for Eoin, who had only ever had women cringe in fear of him and accept his shaft only as a duty, never as a throbbing, aching need. Jude made him feel like he would die without his cock inside him, made Eoin feel like more than his lover, but like his master or his god. As he slid inside his mate, plunging to the hilt with one hard stroke, his other hand wrapped around Jude's own pulsing shaft, and for a split second, he thought he died. In the next, he felt the tingling in his balls, the heat at the base of his spine, and the rush of adrenaline. Instantly he flipped Jude over on his back and pulled him forward, bending his knees, forcing them to his chest as he pounded down into him.

In and out, over and over, he drove into Jude, faster, harder, the only need to be deeper, to feel all of Jude wrapped around him, to be in his lover in every way. When Jude lifted his head, he ground his mouth down over his and kissed him until he couldn't breathe. As Jude dragged in air, Eoin marked him, biting, licking, and sucking until he felt the splash of semen on his abdomen and knew that Jude had found his release. In seconds he followed his mate, flooding his ass with thick, warm fluid. He felt his body trembling hard, almost vibrating over Jude's as he held the man now plastered to his chest.

After long moments spent panting, trying to coax souls so intermingled and tangled that it was hard to tell where each ended and began, back into their bodies, Eoin finally pulled his spent cock from his mate's still tight, fluttering hole. He didn't want to pull out; he could have slept that way, but being so much taller than Jude and wanting the man in his arms, against his heart, Eoin released him only to gather him close and burrow under the blankets. The air in the room was chilled again even with the fire still crackling in the hearth, but Jude was warm; his skin, his breath, and his nude body pressed to Eoin's felt like heaven.

Jude was terrified. How could he have the best sex of his life with a man he barely knew? The sex with Tiernan had been great, but nothing like this. Jude had always held back. He had never been so giving until Eoin. The man made Jude want to throw him down and ride him whenever he saw him. Just Eoin's dark black eyes on him made him hard, and while that was exciting and heart-pounding, what was scary was the rest of it. He felt like he could finally surrender up some of his tightly wound control to another person. He could depend on Eoin. Eoin would be his rock, and that certainty was filling him with thoughts that were new and disturbing as well as warm and solid. Jude, who had never wanted a home, suddenly wanted one desperately.

He could see himself cooking for the man, ironing his shirts, buying vitamins, and going grocery shopping. Even after a year and a half, he had not been ready to live with Tiernan—only an ultimatum made him agree to move in with the man. And look how that had turned out. Jude had come home to find Tiernan fucking Jude's new boss in his bed.

But somehow, Jude knew that Eoin Thral would not end up in bed with anyone else. It was not how the man was made.

Eoin wanted him—only him—and that stirred in Jude a desire to take care of the man, feed him, watch TV with him, go to bed and wake up with him, have him meet his family, have them meet him… his mate… and what did that even *mean*? Were they married in Eoin's eyes? Married in his world? And why did Jude want to be married after only hours spent with the man? What was he doing thinking about two-car garages and kids and retirement plans? He didn't even know Eoin Thral! What made him ready to build his life around him?

A soft snore returned his snowballing thoughts back to Eoin.

"Don't you dare go to sleep," Jude warned him sharply, startling Eoin, who had been so close. How dare he nod off while Jude was having a nervous breakdown! "I have questions for you." Jude sounded slightly unhinged, but he couldn't help it; he was freaking out!

"Are you awake, then, *cairn*?" Eoin asked, trying not to sound irritated. He wanted to sleep.

"Don't call me that, call me Jude."

"I will call you as I like, love."

Jude rolled his eyes before he sat up and looked down at the man. "We need to talk."

"Aye, we do," Eoin agreed, the truth winning out over exhaustion.

"Here you're a man, but in my world you're—"

"I will be a man as well."

Jude squinted down at him. "Wait—what?"

"In whatever form the *cairn* is claimed, so shall the guardian be."

"I'm sorry—what?"

"As you were claimed so shall I remain," Eoin repeated.

"Once again for the learning impaired."

Eoin reached up and put his hand on Jude's cheek, savoring the feel of the smooth skin under his palm. When Jude leaned into the caress, Eoin felt his chest tighten; his heart forgot to beat. Just looking at the man made him so happy.

"I claimed you and so am no longer bound to my beast form on your side of the veil."

The weight of the world lifted off Jude. "Oh yes!" He yelled and the joy on his face made Eoin's heart that had stopped start up again. He was so happy, and Eoin shared all his joy.

Eoin knew that some of the way he was feeling had to do with the fact that the man was his mate, but more of it had to do with Jude himself. The man was amazing. He should have been crumpled up in a ball in the corner, rocking back and forth, crying, and knowing—just *knowing*—that he had lost his mind, but instead Jude was winging it, taking his trip through the veil in stride and keeping his eye on the big picture, which for him, was going home. The revelation that Jude seemed to want to take him home with him pleased Eoin more than he could have ever dreamed. Not that Jude had a choice in the matter; Eoin would never let him go.

"So we can go home, and you can live with me, and you can get a job doing... what do you like to do besides protecting people?"

Another first for Eoin: the first time anyone had ever asked him what he himself liked. No one ever cared; no one ever thought that a guardian could do anything but fight and kill. But Eoin had secrets just like everyone else.

"I can make pieces from wood and metal."

"Art or furniture?"

Eoin could not contain the smile. The ease he felt in Jude's presence was overwhelming; his mate's matter-of-fact acceptance was liberating. "I have made chairs and tables and places for books and chests. I enjoy this work and gave them to the blacksmith to sell at the market."

"And?" Jude prodded him, scooting closer so his hip was against Eoin's side and his hand rested on his chest. "How did they do? Did ya sell anything?"

Eoin nodded. "I sold them all."

"Awesome!" Jude smiled wide. "So you can do that back home with me. We'll rent you a space until you get going and get you into some galleries and see how it goes. I'm in PR, ya know, I can set ya up."

Eoin nodded. "I know not what you said, but your face tells me that you believe I may make this my trade." He swallowed hard. "I would this were so."

Jude stared down into the deep, dark eyes. "I know you have things to do here, and I know that your baroness will not want you to leave with me."

"It is understood that I will leave, Jude Shea. You are my *cairn*, and I will remain forever at your side. The baroness knows this well, and as you are from the other side of the veil, she knows, too, that I will follow you there as I can do no other."

"Tell me what we're gonna do."

"First know that I never planned to keep you here away from your—"

Jude cut him off, "I know. You didn't kidnap me or anything. I know you brought me through the veil to—"

"Make no mistake," Eoin corrected his lover, "'twas my plan to bring you here so that I might claim you as I have done, but know that never would I have kept you here from your kith and kin or from the work that Colton Bale returned to you."

Jude smiled at the mention of his old boss. "It's so weird, but it's like *that's* the dream, ya know, and *this*, right here with you, is the reality."

"Both are real for you, love."

Jude nodded. "I know. It's funny."

Eoin took a breath. "I would never have kept you here against your will. I want only to—"

"You wanna come back with me, right?" Jude asked him sharply, only his tone betraying the fear he felt. What if Eoin had brought him here only as a dalliance and would now send him back through the veil alone?

"Aye, love, 'tis all I want."

"Good," Jude said, releasing a breath he hadn't realized he'd been holding.

Eoin smiled, and his eyes glinted as he looked up at his lover. So close... he was so close to getting Jude to say the words. "I know you want to go home, love. I know you hate Saraso, but I must do my part to make my baroness safe before I take refuge with you."

"I know that."

"You will grant me this time, then?"

"Of course," Jude said, knowing that a man like Eoin would always do what was right for others first and for himself last.

"You will have faith in me, then, even if I am not at your side?"

Wait. "What does that mean?"

Eoin had to explain then that he was going up into the Khal Mountains through the Ellandrel Pass to speak to the leader, the laird, of the outlanders, Crispin Ebudai. It was a mission that would be somewhat perilous. Before Jude could argue with him, Eoin explained that Jude would accompany the baroness and her retinue to the capital city of Goren to meet with the king and try and come to an agreement. Drelindah still had faith in her liege lord and had decided to extend the olive branch of peace before preparing for a siege of her land.

"But I want to go with you," Jude assured Eoin.

"You cannot, for even now there are men prepared to stop us from reaching Crispin."

"You're saying you could be killed?" Jude could hear his voice rising but was powerless to do anything about it.

"All men may be killed, *cairn*." Eoin's voice was gentle. "But I am a guardian, and we are the strongest in all of Midrin."

"Midrin?"

"Aye," Eoin said, his voice low and husky as he looked up at Jude, his hand sliding over Jude's hip, stroking slowly, lazily, not wanting anything but to touch his mate. "Our country is called Midrin. The capital city is Goren, and we live here in Saraso on the land of the Baroness Drelindah Holt."

When he spoke it was full of pride and that made Jude smile.

"Let me tell you of Saraso," Eoin said.

It was unheard of that a woman should carry the title of baroness without there being a baron, but Drelindah's father had made certain—even going so far as to have the seal of the king set to the letters of lineage—that the barony would fall to his only daughter and neither of his sons. He felt, as did everyone else, that she was by far the first and only choice to succeed him as she possessed two traits that neither of her brothers did: she loved the land and she loved the people who lived on it. She was the strongest, bravest person that Eoin Thral knew.

"I liked her right off," Jude told Eoin when he finished his explanation.

"As she did you," he assured his mate. "She looks forward to her trek with you to court."

"How far is it from here?"

"A week in the saddle for you, love." Eoin chuckled evilly. "I am sorry."

Jude groaned miserably. "Some vacation this is."

"Pardon?"

"Never mind."

"Listen, love, for I must tell you what to do if I am killed," Eoin began matter-of-factly. "First—"

"What?" Jude barked at him. "Are you kidding? That's not funny."

Eoin was confused. "I meant not to be a fool, but I must speak to you of—"

"Oh hell, no, I just got you! I don't plan to lose you. I want to fight about what breakfast cereal to buy! I don't want you not breathing."

Eoin shook his head, reaching up and cupping his hand around the back of his mate's neck, easing him down gently to his chest and pulling the blanket up around him. "Love, I want nothing more than to live long at your side, but should I fall in battle, you must know where to turn. Greshan Kai is the domo of Saraso and the guardian of the house of Holt, the protector of us all, the strongest and bravest. He will not fall, and if I do, he has made me an oath of blood to return you to the veil. Should he come for you, you must not fight him but accompany him without question. His word is law. Heard you my words?"

Jude nodded.

"Good."

Taking a quick breath, Jude told Eoin that he wanted to know more about guardians.

"What would you know, then?" Eoin asked, trailing his fingers through Jude's hair, pulling it back gently from his forehead, massaging his scalp at the same time. For so big a man, his touch was tender, reverent, as though Jude were a prize.

"Everything," Jude replied, his eyes drooping.

Eoin gave a heavy sigh as his hand moved to the back of Jude's neck, again massaging gently. "I am a guardian, and we protect the nobility."

"How do you get picked for the job?"

"We are not picked…we are born to be guardians….shifters."

"How'dya mean?"

"When I was born, I was not born an infant, but a dog."

It took Jude a long moment to respond. "I'm sorry?"

"When my mother birthed me, a pup instead of a son, I was brought at once here for the baron and his fenris to train."

"Oh, so they must have known—your parents, I mean—they must have known instantly that you were a guardian." Jude found that interesting. If any woman he knew popped out a dog instead of the baby she was expecting… blessed is not the term that would have been used.

"Aye, so they brought me to Drelindah's father, and he—"

"Wait," Jude said, pulling back to look up into Eoin's face. "What about your parents?"

"What about them, love?"

"What happened to them?"

Broad shoulders shrugged.

"You never knew them?"

"Why would I know them?"

"Shit," Jude breathed. "But then who loved you and took care of you?"

"A guardian is trained; we are not loved."

"But then…." Jude thought about his own mother, who he wanted Eoin to meet, the woman who loved him and his brother more than anything in the world. His mother who always looked forward to seeing him, who made sure the cookies he loved got made every Christmas, and who, when he told her he was gay at eighteen, said okay. His father had a similar reaction. Being gay was not the path he would have chosen for his son, but it did not stop his love; it merely changed who he would expect to accompany Jude to Thanksgiving dinner. The love of his parents was unconditional, and to think of Eoin never being able to experience that made Jude's heart ache. "Oh my God, I'm so sorry."

"As I know not what I have missed, the loss does not touch my heart."

"Are you sure?"

"Aye," Eoin assured his mate.

"Okay," Jude agreed, snuggling back into Eoin's side, molding his body to the bigger man's and wrapping around him.

Eoin understood that he was being comforted because Jude felt sorry for him, and even though he had never, even for a moment, felt sorry for himself, he liked that Jude did. That Jude would care about his feelings, offer sympathy by way of nuzzling against him, ease him with his closeness, Eoin could think of no better sign that the man was falling in love with him. If Jude loved him, it didn't matter if anyone else ever had or would again. The man had felt Eoin's call as soon as he crossed over the veil, had put himself in mortal danger to save him, and now accepted the knowledge that Eoin was a guardian… Eoin could think of no greater gift than to be the owner of Jude's heart. It was all he wanted.

Eoin cleared his throat before it closed with a surge of emotion. "What else would you know?"

"Just talk," Jude told him, lifting his chin to kiss Eoin's jaw.

Jude's lips were so very soft. Even as tired as he was, as sated and warm and content, he felt the faint stirring of arousal skitter over his skin and hot blood rush to his groin. For a man who could normally go weeks without sex, the new raw needs of his body were an epiphany.

"Eoin?"

"Oh, well, as I said we are born animals, not men, and there are none who will have us."

"How do you mean 'have'?"

"We are animals, beasts, and no other but our mate will have us without coin or force. None of us that live on Drelindah's land have ever raped women, but there are others I have known that have."

"But there are women who are paid to sleep with guardians."

Eoin didn't ask how Jude knew that; he was too distracted by the lips that nibbled along his jaw to his ear and were now tracing some invisible path down the side of his neck. The bites, so sensual and hot, were one thing, but the fact that Jude could not seem to help himself was the greater revelation. His mate wanted him—found him desirable—and Eoin, having never believed anyone would, was overwhelmed. Jude Shea was a wonder to him.

"Hey, you stopped talking."

Eoin cleared his throat as Jude's tongue slid over his collarbone.

"You all right?" Jude asked, leaning back to look at his mate. "You made a funny noise."

The guardian was certain he had made a strange noise, perhaps a strangled one. Jude was in peril of being flat on his back in moments if he didn't cease the delicious torture.

"Are there a lot of guardians?"

"Nae," Eoin answered, his voice raspy, "and as there are only few of us born, so is the same true for our mates... only one for every guardian."

"Oh."

"If we sense not our mate by the time we pass our eighteenth summer, then is it understood that we will not find one. Perhaps the mate was killed or died... we may never know," Eoin said quietly. "There are others who believe that, for some, our mates lie beyond the veil."

"Did you?"

"I did not. I had thought to never have a mate as crossing the veil at all seemed folly."

"Why?"

"What if I never found my mate and was then alone far from home?"

Having a debate with Eoin about why it was always good to take chances seemed to Jude a waste of time so instead he asked the more practical question plaguing him.

"So why doesn't everyone who hates it here just cross the veil?"

"I miss your meaning."

"I mean why don't tons of unhappy citizens cross over the veil into my world?"

"None but guardians and those who travel with a guardian may pass through the veil. If one is but a man he might search in vain for a lifetime and never find the entrance."

"I don't understand."

"Let us say that you would leave me....you may run from this place to your world, but without me you can never come again to mine. Veilers, as you are called, may return from where a guardian has once taken you, but you cannot come back to us if you chose to."

The words saddened Jude for reasons he didn't understand, but he kept the conversation light. "So even your king couldn't go without a guardian?"

"Aye, and as the king does not believe in the veil, he would never think to make such a journey."

"What? How do you not believe in something that actually exists?"

"The veil is...." Eoin searched for the words. "The veil is as alive as you or I. It allows or denies passage for reasons we know not."

"That makes no sense. You're saying it's like a portal that works when it feels like it."

"Aye, and that is why the king does not believe. If I told you that something was there, and when you went you could neither see the evidence nor touch it, you, too, would cease to believe."

"So the veil works only sometimes. We might not be able to make it back."

"You belong there; so you will always be able to journey back. I will be with you, so I, too, will return. But others.... The men who followed me through the veil when you first came upon me, if should they try again, I doubt that they would be able to follow."

"Why?"

"I know not."

Jude shifted in the bed, away from his lover so that he could see his face. "You think it's, like, presumptuous for you to think you have the veil figured out, 'cause you're just a lowly guardian, huh?" Jude smiled at him, which made Eoin's breath catch.

"Aye." Eoin nodded, loving the wicked grin and mischievous glint in his mate's eyes.

"Just tell me, dog boy."

Eoin's eyes widened as the words sank in. *What had he...?* "Dog boy?"

Jude giggled, and Eoin grabbed him and wrapped his arms around him before pinching his ass hard. His mate wiggling in his embrace was causing Eoin's pulse to race, his groin to throb, and a quickening deep inside him. His reaction to Jude astounded him. Would it always be this way or only now when it was so new?

"Tell me what you're thinking," Jude said breathlessly before he dissolved into soft laughter again.

Eoin just wanted to hold his mate. "I believe that the veil allowed Cuyler Adon and the other gryphons to follow me—"

"I saw dogs attacking you that night—that means other guardians were—"

"You saw what you wanted to see," Eoin assured him, smoothing a hand down Jude's back, reveling in the feeling of the warm, silken skin, the bumpy spine, and the curve that flowed into the firm, round ass.

"I saw dogs."

"You saw gryphons, as that is what they were—but as your mind had ne'er seen a gryphon, you believe you saw dogs."

Jude was almost positive that he had seen dogs, but it had been dark, and he'd seen them only briefly, so maybe.... "So you're saying that those guys, the gryphons that were attacking you, that was Cuyler and the other guys?"

"Aye, they chased me through the veil."

"And because they were with you, they got to go through."

Eoin nodded.

"And if they lost you, they couldn't get back."

"Aye."

"I wonder how they… I mean, what did they do for money or clothes or—"

"Better for us not to know, as they are men or gryphons but not dogs." Eoin sighed. "A dog, as you yourself know, may be taken in and cared for, but a gryphon…. We can only hope that few lives were touched by them."

"You think they killed people."

"I can fathom no other end."

Jude nodded. The thought was sobering. "So when we go back, we'll go alone. We're not gonna bring anyone else through."

"Aye."

Jude was silent for several minutes, just thinking. "So what if after living with me for a while, you get sick of it and you wanna come back here?"

Eoin breathed in his mate's warm musky scent, buried his face in Jude's hair, and spoke from his soul. "Of you I will never be done, love."

Jude felt like he had been punched in the stomach. The words were true; he knew it. He felt it. He had absolute faith in Eoin's unwavering, unchangeable heart. The man loved him. "Shit," Jude swore.

"Love?"

"Sorry." Jude dragged in a deep breath. "You should go to sleep; you have a hard day ahead of you tomorrow."

"As do you, love."

"All I hafta do is sit on a horse. You might hafta actually kill somebody."

"Only those who attack me first will die," Eoin said as he yawned and turned Jude in his arms so that they were spooned together before he closed his eyes.

"That's right." Jude chuckled softly. "You're a badass."

Eoin grunted, drifting toward sleep, more content than he had ever been in his life even though he had no clue what Jude had just said.

"Do you even care that I was starving and that if the girls hadn't brought me any food, I'd still be starving?"

"Pardon?" Eoin asked irritably, having been so close to sleep. "What girls do you speak of?"

Jude smiled over the fact that he had gotten a rise out of the man and explained about first, Kennis coming to the room to sleep with Eoin, and then about the others coming back with her later. The wine, Jude told him, had been really good. It turned out that Eoin didn't give a damn that Jude had been starving, but the girls in his room were an issue. It was very telling.

"Kennis is a whore. You are not allowed in her company unattended."

"Oh, no?"

"Heard you my words, Jude Shea?" Eoin asked, his voice rising.

"She wanted to fuck me."

There was that word again that rolled Eoin's insides. "I am the only one that will *fuck* you," he growled before he bit down lightly on Jude's shoulder. "I will kill any other I find in your bed, Jude Shea, mark my words."

But Jude knew bravado when he heard it. Eoin might be a big tough guardian, but if he ever caught Jude cheating on him, he would simply turn his back and walk away, his heart too broken to fight, only able to grieve.

"Am I speaking plain to you, then?"

"I got it."

"Do you, now?"

Jude smiled, but Eoin couldn't see it in the encroaching darkness. The fire was getting smaller and the room colder, so Jude scooted closer to his lover. "You won't hafta kill anybody. There's nobody else I want."

His words moved Eoin that much closer to the ones he wanted to hear more than anything: that Jude loved him. If Jude would sleep with no one else, would allow no other in his bed, then he was in love… he just didn't know it yet. Perhaps time apart would be a good thing, allowing Jude to see how much he would miss Eoin.

"Why did you not go to the kitchen if you were hungry?"

Like Jude knew where the kitchen was. Like it even mattered anymore. "Go to sleep," Jude murmured.

"If only you would still your tongue, I might, Jude Shea."

"I thought you liked my tongue."

Eoin groaned almost painfully. On the one hand, his body demanded rest, but on the other, it was clearly responding to Jude's wicked and enticing words. His mate was wanton, and the knowledge flamed through Eoin like a brushfire.

Jude wiggling his ass harder against Eoin's groin was not helping him settle in for sleep, but when Jude let his head fall to the side so Eoin's chin could notch into the side of his neck and pulled Eoin's arm across his chest, carnal thoughts were drowned under a wave of emotion. Jude moved as though he had always slept in the circle Eoin's arms, inviting the closeness. The feeling of belonging rose up in Eoin, and he clenched his jaw against the onslaught. He held his mate tight even as he followed Jude into sleep.

Chapter Seven

DRELINDAH HOLT wanted more than anything to speak to Eoin's mate, but she kept her distance and made certain everyone else did as well, because she knew the man was overwhelmed and needed time to adjust. She watched him on the mare that Eoin had insisted he take, an older, gentle creature that could not outrun other horses but would neither spook easily nor throw her rider. He wanted Jude's journey to the castle to be uneventful in every way. Drelindah understood and was, in fact, impressed with her guardian. She knew, too, that his time with her had ended. He would follow his mate back through the veil and be lost to her forever.

While it saddened her, the loss of a loyal and trusted friend, she was brimming over with happiness for him. So long had she seen only emptiness in him, a vacant look in his eyes, a distance in his manner; he had been a vessel filled only with duty. But when he had returned to her, she saw the change immediately. Those eyes were charged with fire, his manner was decisive, and the way he had bolted from the room when they had all finished talking, securing their plans… that had been most telling. He craved his mate, and Drelindah was thrilled. Eoin Thral deserved to be loved—all her men did—but Eoin most of all. She hoped Jude Shea would care for his heart.

Drelindah wanted to talk to Jude, to gauge his feelings for her guardian, but instead she waited, knowing she had nothing but time. The journey would be long and boring; her only hope for excitement was Jude. He needed to stop thinking so hard and engage with the others. It was time to cast off his gloom and enjoy the journey.

Jude was miserable. He had been pulled from a dreamless sleep, dragged from a warm cozy bed, and tossed into an icy lake. It was Eoin's morning regimen, the one he followed each day, and he had seen no reason why Jude would not do the same. But the man was a hardened warrior and Jude was a creative director at a PR firm. When Jude had roared out his indignation, Eoin had understood that perhaps, in the future, a little finesse might be in order. Jude's leg had cramped up seconds later, and Eoin had been forced to save him from drowning. This was all before the sun had even risen. So when Jude had sat shivering on the bank of the lake, teeth chattering, trying to rub the knot out of his foot and calf, it had still been too dark to see clearly. But then he had felt Eoin's strong hands on him, sighed deeply when he was transferred into the warm cocoon of Eoin's arms, and settled back against the man's chest and into his lap. When Eoin kissed the bridge of his nose, his eyes had drifted closed, content.

Eoin had tried to get up a few minutes later, announcing that it would be dawn soon and they had to leave. Jude had asked, had pleaded to go with him, only to be adamantly turned down. What Eoin could not turn down was Jude's demand to be made love to. When Jude had kissed him breathless, twining his tongue with Eoin's, it had Eoin clutching at Jude's skin, pulling Jude's legs around him, and seating himself deep inside his love. Eoin was lost.

"Let me go with you," Jude had panted.

Eoin hadn't been able to think; all he could focus on was the man riding him, how beautiful Jude had looked doing it, the way Jude had risen and lowered, his own cock sliding in and out of Eoin's hand, Jude's ass taking in the long, hard, thick length of him.

Eoin's mate was trying to kill him.

Later as Eoin had lain beside him, chest heaving, having roared out his pleasure, even then had Jude pressed him to be allowed to remain at his side. Eoin had been impressed with Jude's single-mindedness, but not enough to allow him to make the trip. He had enjoyed having Jude hurl a boot at him in frustration.

As he rode out of the keep with the others, Eoin's last sight of Jude was of him smiling. The idea that Jude, his mate—as uncertain and frightened as Eoin knew he must be—was making sure that Eoin remembered him as happy warmed the big man's heart.

"I had wondered at the choice of the gods to give you a male mate," Arius said as they rode toward the woods. "But seeing him there to farewell you… I find no flaw in the union."

Eoin smiled over at the chief counselor of the baroness, and the other man nodded before looking away. Eoin wondered now, hours later, how Jude was faring with his tender backside on the endless road.

Jude needed the time to think and was pleased that no one tried to talk to him. He had a new mate, boyfriend, lover…? He wasn't sure exactly what Eoin was, but he knew what the man wanted to be. Eoin wanted to be his husband. He wanted them to be married, and in spite of how completely weird everything was, Jude was pretty sure he wanted the same thing. Leave it to him to find the one person in existence who believed in monogamy as much as he did. His friends were going to freak out.

It was so odd to think about his life, his real life, full of e-mails and lattes and hot showers. He couldn't wait to get back even as he realized that he was worried about Eoin really being able to leave this life behind. How could he ask him to do that? It was so much to consider, but all he really had was time.

IT WAS only supposed to take four days to reach the castle, but Jude was certain he wasn't going to make it. If he never saw another horse in his life, it would be too soon. No wonder cowboys were bowlegged! Throughout the day, the only bright spot he could find was talking to Drelindah. It was certainly not even worth attempting a conversation with one of her stoic guardians.

Of the six shifters that lived on Drelindah's land along with their fenris Drist, only two, Orim and Vardeen, traveled with the baroness. The mistress of Saraso had left Greshan Kai at her holding to keep it safe and had sent Drist up the mountain to Crispin Ebudai along with Eoin, Lazoore and Arius. Jude wished of course that Eoin might have accompanied her instead but even Drist or Greshan might have spoken to him. As it was, between Orim and Vardeen, not a word was uttered. Jude considered himself lucky to have Drelindah.

She was fun to hang out with, and he had dredged secrets from her in the course of only one morning and afternoon that no one else knew. She had surprised herself with the confidences she shared as they rode side by side. Jude's favorite was that she had fallen very hard for Crispin Ebudai, the leader of the outlanders. Since her land bordered his, they had to speak often. They had men who guarded the Ellandrel pass together. It was the only route in or out of the mountains.

"So your men watch his, and his watch yours." Jude gave her a knowing smile, looking over at her. "How nice."

"This was how it began, but as the pass has been guarded for so long, all the men are well acquainted by now and call each other kin."

Jude nodded.

Drelindah sighed, deeply unaware that Jude was counting all the times she did that as she talked about anything pertaining to Crispin Ebudai.

"It's nice that everybody gets along. Your men, his men. It would make things kind of easy if you wanted to put them all together," Jude offered suggestively.

It took a minute for his words and the intonation to sink in. When they did, Drelindah gasped. "What? Jude Shea, what do you speak of?" She moved so abruptly, sitting up in her saddle, that she spooked her horse. It took several pats and soft words to soothe the stallion.

"Oh, please." He laughed at her. "Like you never thought about it. Any other guy you hook up with, he becomes the baron; but this guy, Crispin whatever, he's already got a job, so you stay baroness alone, and he keeps his title, but you guys get to sleep together every night. It sounds like a plan to me—is he hot?"

Drelindah's breath caught before she leaned sideways and swatted him on the arm. "How dare you even suggest such—"

"Talk, woman!" He laughed harder. "Tell me what the man looks like."

Apparently, from her lengthy, halting description, Crispin was some sort of blond god with the clearest, brightest, bluest eyes ever bestowed on a man. Jude rolled his eyes after the long, rambling description of the man's considerable charms were detailed for him.

"Oh, for crissakes," he groaned, "how bad have you got it for this guy?"

"Jude Shea, how dare—"

Jude cut her off. "Does he like you?"

Drelindah's brows furrowed. "He suggested at our last parlay that to seal the new land parcel between us that he take me to his bed."

"Oh yeah," Jude chuckled as her eyes flicked to his. "I'm gonna go with yeah—he likes ya."

"Perhaps he speaks these honeyed words to all the women he beds."

"Yeah? You get that vibe from him that he's a player?"

Her brow furrowed. "I have no—"

"You think he's got a lot of women in his bed?"

She shivered with memory. "He spoke to me that there were no others… he wants but one."

"And?" Jude prodded. He just couldn't resist; it was too good. "Who's the one?"

She bit her lip, and with that Jude knew that the scary Baroness of Saraso had it bad for Crispin Ebudai. Jude gave her a flashing grin.

"So whatcha gonna do there, lady? You gonna let him marry some scary outland bitch or are you gonna fuck his brains out and keep him?"

"I know not the words you spoke but that their intent was filthy."

Jude waggled his eyebrows at her. "You're gonna secure his passage right into your bed. Nice, I like your style."

She was back to being horrified, and Jude dissolved into laughter as he flushed bright pink. He would help her if he could; he knew more now about what would secure her happiness than even her closest advisors.

At nightfall they made camp, and Jude was so happy to be off the horse he did a little dance. As it was nothing anyone there had ever seen, a little Cabbage Patch with some Running Man thrown in, he stopped before someone decided he needed to be put out of his misery.

"Come, Jude," Drelindah said as she smiled at him, "let me show you where… your tent…." She trailed off, looking around, her eyes narrowing as she listened.

"What's wrong?"

She lifted her hand to quiet him. She was almost certain she had heard sounds behind her in the woods, but that was impossible. The perimeter of the camp was secured and her men, her guardians, were close at hand. But it was dark; there were no fires, the braziers that were burning under shelters were giving off more smoke than light. Pulling back the hood on her riding cape, letting the light rain dampen her hair, she listened again. The whinny of a horse made her run.

"Jude!" She grabbed his hand even as the horsemen broke from the tree line and rode through camp. There was screaming and shouting, and she ran on, needing to get to her tent, to her bow.

"Baroness!"

The shout turned her head, Vardeen running toward her, Orim charging in the opposite direction, chasing men away from her.

"No!"

Drelindah turned and saw one of her waiting women almost trampled by a man on horseback and was more stunned than anything else. Why did the man not stop and scoop up the buxom courtier and carry her off into the night? Why was he only riding toward her? Quickly she cleared her head and ran on, veering toward her tent. The ringing of steel was deafening around her, but she heard a yell. Lifting her head, she saw the man barreling toward her.

She understood her peril too late as an arm wrapped around her waist and she was lifted off her feet and thrown across a saddle. But just as fast as she was there, she was sprawled on the ground on top of Jude. He had wrenched her from the man's grip, but the force had sent her tumbling into him, hurling him backward into the dirt.

"Christ," Jude groaned, winded and sore. "Get off me! You weigh a ton."

She would take him to task about his disparaging tone and remark about her weight later. For now, he had saved her, and there was no time to even think—only act.

Jude lurched sideways as hooves tried to trample him, and with the surge of adrenaline through him, he rolled to his feet in front of the baroness. Grabbing her wrist, he yanked her after him and ran for the tree line.

Branches whipped at his face and hair, and he had to shield his eyes with his forearm in front of him as the rain that had been a mist moments before became a downpour. He had no idea where he was going, and Drelindah had either forgotten that he wasn't from around there or she was too frantic to care. Either way, they ran together through the dense forest until a roar of water made Jude freeze in his tracks. Drelindah could not stop her momentum, but he held tight and whipped her back around into his arms. They stood plastered together, panting, both trying to listen over the pounding of their hearts.

"What is that?"

Drelindah tried to catch her breath enough to speak. "I believe us near the Cinnian Falls. 'Tis a drop to our death, Jude Shea, should we run any further."

He turned to go back as he saw the glint of a sword in the darkness. A man was hacking his way through the trees and brush to reach them.

"Drelindah Holt, we have you surrounded! Stay your flight!"

Jude had no intention of *staying* anything. Instead he grabbed Drelindah's hand, bolted forward, and yanked her after him. "I was a lifeguard all through college," he yelled as they ran. "I went to school on a swimming scholarship, and I even played water polo."

Drelindah had no idea what he was talking about. "I want my men!"

"Your men aren't here! They're back with the others," he told her, hoping to focus her on what they could do to save themselves instead of waiting for her guardians to show up and rescue them. "We have to jump."

"No!"

"If we survive the fall, I promise you won't drown!"

"I cannot swim, Jude Shea," she yelled back.

Hadn't he already covered that? "Don't worry," he called out, "just don't let go of me."

She heard Jude's instruction as they ran off the side of the cliff:

"Whatever happens don't… let… go…!"

Winian Anek, brother of Jaan Anek, servant of Bishop Rista Dumal, could not stop in time, and so followed Jude and Drelindah to what his men believed was certain death. Even so, Winian's second in command, Braedhn Sron, ordered his troops to search the banks of the roaring, winding river that the heaving, pounding waterfall poured into. The drop was easily fifty feet, and there were enormous sharp rocks at the bottom. If they found any remains at all, they would be only pieces. There was no hope that the baroness or Winian or the servant had survived.

What had possessed the baroness to make such a desperate leap to keep from captivity, Braedhn could not fathom. Didn't she know that they meant her no harm? Didn't she know that their only task was to keep her safe? Why had the foolish woman killed herself and taken a servant and Winian Anek to a watery grave with her? It was all so unnecessary.

In a tangle of limbs, Drelindah and Jude fell together through the dark night into the frigid, foaming waterfall. It was like a whiplash of ice and pain as they were inside the wall of water driven blindly down, then flying through the darkness, and then suddenly hit by a blast of hot air from the side of the mountain. The gas trapped underground leaked from the earth in several places, one close to the base of the waterfall. It was like diving into an enormous Jacuzzi jet.

As Jude and Drelindah were sent flying out away from the side of the mountain, hurtling into the river, she screamed and he let out a war whoop of joy. Jude had a second to feel the flood of relief before he hit the glacial water. Exploding moments later through the surface, Jude was sure that he had never been so cold in his life. It didn't matter that he had no idea what frostbite felt like; he was still certain he had it.

Drelindah Holt took gulping swallows of water as she was tossed in the waves, pulled under, and caught in the current. To her it was a hard tug, to Jude, having swum in Hawaii in *real* current, there was no comparison. He reached for her, drew her to him, and tucked her tightly to his chest. She was so thankful for his warmth that she burst into tears.

"You're okay," he assured her gently.

Drelindah was trembling, her teeth were chattering, and she basically felt like a girl. A needy, scared girl, and she hated it. She was a baroness; she needed to act like one.

"Cut yourself some slack." Jude chuckled and started swimming toward shore. "You just jumped off a waterfall, all right?"

She nodded, and when her feet touched sand at her feet, she started to cry again. When Jude heard the gasp behind them, he looked out toward the darkness. The full moon was helpful, but it was still tough to see anything, though the downpour had subsided to a drizzle. The sound of someone choking before a second gasp confirmed Jude's worst suspicions. There was someone out there in the deadly cold water who needed saving. Rising fast, Jude bolted back toward the water, hurling himself like a spear into the heaving river.

Winian Anek was being dragged down by the current, submerged, and tumbled around, and finally, between his armor and his exertions, he was spent. Sinking under the water for the final time, he could no longer hold his breath and inhaled the frigid liquid in gulps.

Jude dove deep, hoping that even as tired as the man or woman was, fighting for life in the freezing water, that there was still enough strength to resist being swept downstream. In the dark and without a cry for help to guide him, Jude's chances of success were small.

It was peaceful, Winian thought as his eyes closed, and he only regretted not dying in battle as his father had before him.

Jude's lungs screamed, his muscles throbbed with painful spasms, and he was cold down to his bones, but still he searched with his hands in the inky darkness. The relief when his fingers closed on armor almost, literally, drowned him. He was careful not to gasp underwater.

When Winian was pulled from the river minutes later, he was unconscious.

Drelindah watched in interest even as she sat crouched and shivering beside the two men. Jude worked fast, yanking off the chain mail the other man was wearing to reach his chest. She had no idea what Jude planned to do. The soldier was dead, drowned; there was nothing to do but leave him and run. But Jude was working hard, rolling his charge sideways as some water drained from his mouth before returning him to his back and starting chest compressions. Pushing and counting, he pinched off Winian's nose as he leaned his chin back and exhaled between the blue lips. Again, over and over for several minutes, Jude was so focused on the man, committed to saving his life that mounted soldiers were able to surround him and Drelindah without him noticing. Drelindah noticed and was terrified, but she was also surprised that the men did nothing to stop Jude. They just watched him, knowing, too, that Winian was dead but unable to stop the man from trying to revive him.

It took only minutes but felt to Jude like an eternity before he was able to push the water from Winian's lungs. Jude started to panic, afraid that even after pulling the man from the river that in the end it would not be enough. When Jude was rewarded for his efforts and the air that he had breathed into Winian brought him choking, coughing, and heaving back to consciousness, he was momentarily overcome. After several long moments in which Winian Anek could only lay still and stare up at his savior, he finally sat up, much to the collective surprise of those around him. Seconds later, a cheer went up as Winian stared wide-eyed at Jude.

"You're a healer," Drelindah said with so much awe in her voice that Jude turned his head to look at her.

"I was a lifeguard for four years," he corrected her, smiling.

She ignored his comment completely. "I had no idea my guardian had mated a healer."

"You're the mate of a guardian?" Winian croaked.

"I am," Jude said as his eyes welled up with tears. The adrenaline rush finally subsiding, between running for his life and saving a man's life, Jude was overwhelmed. He needed to be grounded and in that moment when he felt vulnerable and unsure, his mind conjured up the huge beautiful man who was his lover and Jude felt a blanket of calm envelop him.

Once they were back in the real world, Jude had no idea what would happen at work. He was unsure if the opportunity would still be there when he finally got home—if he got home—but what he did know was that with Eoin at his side, he would no longer be alone. There would be other jobs, but no other man. He needed Eoin Thral because he loved him. At that moment everything made sense.

"We are the private guard of Rista Dumal; he sent us to intercept the Baroness of Saraso and take her to the holding of Crispin Ebudai. He fears that if she is seen by the king, she will see only the inside of his dungeon."

Well, everything except the words of the man Jude had just saved from drowning.

Jude looked at Drelindah. "So we're not going to see the king?"

From her open-mouthed expression Jude guessed that she was as confused as he was.

He turned back to the man. "I'm sorry, but Drelindah wants to see the king. She needs to try and talk some sense into him."

"'Tis much too late for that. The king has called for the head of Drelindah Holt, as she has been charged with treason."

"Treason for what?" Jude asked before Drelindah could.

Winian Anek took a deep breath, savoring the air in his lungs, the crisp breeze on his face, and the fact that he was chilled to the bone instead of dead. "Drelindah Holt is charged with treason for joining forces with Crispin Ebudai and Bishop Dumal to overthrow the monarchy."

It was then that Drelindah started to scream.

Chapter Eight

SHE was seething. Jude watched her stalk from one end of the tent to the other and didn't even try to offer any words of comfort. Instead, he picked at the pieces of deer meat, chunks of what he thought might be rye bread, and what looked like grapes. They were sweet like grapes, and there were no seeds. The quince tea was good, but again, he didn't offer Drelindah any. She was too busy fuming.

"I am a fool! I was so blinded by the eyes of the man and his form and his words... how could I miss that he and the bishop were planning to overthrow the king?"

She shouted the last part, and Jude gave her a reassuring smile.

"It was all a trap set in motion seasons ago, and I had no thought other than my own desires. What a fool I am!"

He chuckled. "You are being way too hard on yourself, and we both know you have never been a fool in your life."

She was struck by the absolute sincerity of his words.

"Do ya think maybe you should keep an open mind until you see the people on Crispin Ebudai's land? I mean, Winian said that—"

"I care not what Winian said! The man is a snake and—"

"Did I hear my name?" the man in question asked as he strode into the enormous tent, the flap held open for him by one of the two guards watching the only way in or out.

"I demand that you release us! I am a baroness!"

But Winian Anek had no eyes or ears for the Baroness of Saraso; he was there to see Jude. His men had told him how Jude had saved him, had pressed lips to his, and had breathed life into him. It was an image that Winian Anek could not drive from his mind.

"Hey." Jude smiled up at him.

The man's lack of fear in his presence was overwhelming for the soldier. "Are you warm?" Winian asked, crossing to Jude, squatting down in front of him, and looking into his face. "Do you have enough to eat?"

"Yeah, we do, thanks." Jude nodded, sitting up. "How do you feel?"

"I am well, Jude Shea," he said, having asked Jude what his name was as they rode back to his camp. "You made certain I would be."

Jude's eyes locked on his. "And you kept your word about not hurting the baroness, so we're even."

"No, I still owe you my life."

Jude sighed, tiredness for his earlier exertions starting to creep up on him. "That's okay."

He spoke so oddly, but as Winian did not believe in the veil, he thought Jude from the colonies or farther away, perhaps from across the wild Seruan Sea. He noticed suddenly the cuts on Jude's fingers. "What have you done?"

Jude shrugged. "Your chain mail stuff is sharp, and I got sliced up taking it off."

"We should bandage them."

"No, it's fine," Jude sighed, the warm velvety sound of his voice seeping into Winian.

He sat and watched the light from the flickering flames dance over Jude's face, cast golden light on his skin, and kiss his eyes. "You are a fearless man."

Jude gave out a snort of laughter. "Hardly."

"And yet you swam out for me, knowing that had I died, my men would have cut you down."

"That thought never entered my mind, actually."

"Were you afraid of nothing?"

"The only thing I was afraid of was that you were gonna die."

Winian stared into Jude's drooping eyes. "Indeed."

Jude gave him a lopsided grin. "How long will it take to get up the mountain?"

"Two, perhaps three days," Winian answered, watching Jude, studying him, looking for and not finding even a flicker of fear in him. It was amazing to behold, because everyone feared Winian; they cringed when he spoke, flinched when he moved his hands too fast, or winced simply from his nearness... all except Jude. After saving his life, the man had helped him to his feet, drawn his arms across his shoulders when they walked, and made sure he was securely on his horse before walking away. Never in Winian's adult life had anyone been concerned about him save his own family.

"Winian?"

Brought from his thoughts, he found himself again faced with the most beautiful eyes he had ever seen. Brown, flecked with gold. Who knew eyes could even be that color?

"If Drelindah and I just go back to Saraso, can we go?"

"No, we have orders to take the baroness up the mountain to Crispin. The bishop ordered us to see to her safety. She must not be lost."

Jude looked over at Drelindah. "It looks like you're gonna see Crispin's land."

She jerked her hand at Winian. "And I am to do what—trust my safety to this dreg?"

Jude smiled at her. "I have no idea what a dreg is, but you can trust Winian."

"How can you be certain?"

"You said yourself he works for the bishop, and the bishop wants you safe, so if Winian works for him, then he wants to keep you safe too."

Drelindah's dark blue eyes flicked to Winian's green ones.

Winian rose to his feet under her scrutiny, taking a breath as he did, making sure that the flush of excitement he felt didn't show on his features. Jude had faith in him, in his integrity, and he didn't even *know* him. The knowledge was captivating, Jude himself was refreshing, open, honest, and without a doubt, appealing. The man with his ripe lips and bewitching eyes was very, very appealing. Having had many men in and out of his bed over the years as well as a parade of women, Winian Anek was quite a connoisseur of beauty.

And Jude had all the qualities of a woman, smooth skin, full lips, and a grace of moment as well as the strength, athleticism, and build of a man. Winian could find no flaw in his savior, and that combined with Jude's blind faith was overwhelming.

"I will wait," Drelindah said slowly, her voice sharp, "and I will see the people you say the king has hurt, see the land, and hear the words of Crispin Ebudai."

Winian nodded and looked back at Jude, who gave him a quick smile.

"We've got your word you're gonna protect her, right?" Jude checked.

"Aye," Winian breathed, "you have my word, Jude Shea."

"What are the words of a dreg worth?" Drelindah spat out.

Jude widened his eyes when he looked at her, and she threw her hands up.

"As you say," she groused, clearly exasperated. "I will take his word."

Winian looked back and forth between his two prisoners. "She trusts you."

"Why wouldn't she? I'm a good guy. So are you. We're fine."

The soldier had heard stories about the temper of the Baroness of Saraso; they had all told him that going to fetch the Ice Witch, as she was called, would be a bloody affair. As no one had known the calming effect that Jude Shea would have on her, they had not counted on it. As Winian watched the Baroness of Saraso sit down beside Jude and lean into his side, he had hope suddenly that all his leader's plans might actually come to fruition. If the baroness listened and could be convinced of the truth, then the bloody reign of King Reis Paradoon might finally come to an end. If only she could be reasoned with, all would be well. Perhaps with Jude at her side, all the pieces would finally fall into place.

Watching Jude talking to the baroness, their heads bent together, her arm wrapped around his knee, her eyes dropping closed as she still listened to him, Winian knew this was the best chance they would ever have to convince the strongest woman in all of Midrin that she was on the wrong side. It was his last thought before he bid the two people who were no longer paying any attention to him good evening.

Chapter Nine

THE trip up the mountain took twice as long as Winian had anticipated because every time he took the time to point out a survivor of one of the King's atrocities, Drelindah Holt dismounted at once to speak to the man or woman he had pointed out. It was exhausting. She would sit in homes, small cottages that dotted the mountain side, and listen and ask questions. Jude had taken to writing down the accounts, drawing pictures to accompany them and, of course, recording names. And while for Winian it was satisfying to hear his version of events corroborated, the process of people just talking about their lives took hours and sometimes days off their travel time. There was no way to complain, however, as it was all happening exactly as Crispin Ebudai and Bishop Dumal had hoped.

Unfortunately, the more time Winian's men spent with Drelindah and Jude, the more they became at ease in their presence. He watched daily as looks from his soldiers became orders, orders became words, words became sentences, and from there it was banter and stories and laughter. No amount of his warnings for his men to keep on their guard worked, and especially not with Jude.

That evening as he stood close to the fire, Winian watched as Drelindah and Jude sat at the eating tables with his men and talked. Two of his soldiers sat shoulder-to-shoulder with Jude, another poured water for the baroness. How was he supposed to keep a division when everyone was already friendly?

"Jude tended the sick last set," Winian's second-in-command Braedhn told him walking around in front of his leader to stand at his side. "You need to rein he and the baroness in before all the men follow them back to Saraso."

"We are outlanders now; they would not leave," Winian said, turning to look at his second-in-command. "Is that not so?"

Braedhn narrowed his eyes. "The baroness is a woman and a leader, so they feel the desire to both protect and bed her; her man Jude is a healer, and he listens far more than he speaks. I cannot name any of your men who are not already snared in their web."

Winian couldn't either, himself included.

"I will make her mine if she stays much longer," Braedhn said, watching Drelindah laugh at something one of the men said.

"And I will keep the healer," Markus, another of Winian's men, said as he walked by his leader and his second-in-command, "if I can best Niall for him."

"Niall," Winian turned to face Markus.

He shrugged. "It seems your shield-bearer has taken a liking to the healer, follows him about like a dog... even now, look there. He's found him.

Winian's eyes returned to Jude and finding him, spied Niall. He saw the huge soldier tousle Jude's hair, his hand lingering in the dark curls, watching the silky hair run through his fingers.

"What say you?" Markus chuckled, smiling at Braedhn.

Winian turned back to him. "Pardon?"

"He baits me, not you," Braedhn told him, and Winian noticed the wicked grin.

"I say again: We leave Crispin Ebudai to his destiny, and I will claim the healer and you the baroness. What say you, Braedhn Sron?"

Winian chose to ignore the suggestion that his men were going to desert and instead walked over to Drelindah and Jude. Her face lit up when she saw him, the smile genuine and her eyes soft. Stunned, he smiled back when she playfully smacked his arm. She liked him. His mind reeled as she giggled, enjoying his dumbfounded expression. When in the name of the five gods had that happened? When had her anger and outrage changed to genuine affection?

"Hey," Jude said. He exhaled slowly. "Why don't you sit down and talk to us?"

And the invitation, for no ulterior motive was irresistible. When he took a seat beside Jude, the man bumped him with his shoulder before returning to the conversation he was engaged in. And even if Winian said nothing, it was understood that he was included. Drelindah's smiling glances, Jude's proximity; it was too much for a man who lived a stoic, Spartan existence. How could he hold up against Drelindah's trust and Jude's warmth? What in the name of all that was holy was he supposed to do?

THE trek up the mountain became, in Jude's mind, a goodwill mission. There was a barn raising and displaced people joining the caravan, mostly women and children, and Winian felt more than ever that Drelindah was in charge and not him. The baroness changed his plans, countered his orders, and dismissed him often with a wave of her hand. Winian would stand there stunned as his own soldiers raced to do her bidding. She was a baroness, after all. Always Jude was there beside him to cushion the blow and give him a little pat of reassurance. It was almost condescending, and Winian wondered if somehow that was how Jude meant it.

DAYS later Drelindah Holt, Baroness of Saraso, rode over the drawbridge into Castle Ithrum, stronghold of Crispin Ebudai, laird of the outlanders, and was surprised at the welcome she received. The bridge was lined with colored lanterns, musicians, and hundreds of children strewing flower petals in their path as they passed.

All along the route to the castle there had been similar demonstrations of joy. The people welcomed the baroness with open arms as it was her holding that guarded the pass that led to the mountains. If she was finally with them, if she and their laird were united in kinship, then all the years of covert warfare were finally behind them. As blossoms rained from the sky, strewn from the battlements by shouting crowds, Drelindah was touched by her reception.

Passing under the first gatehouse, which was two of the outer towers connected together, Jude looked up and saw guards staring down at the procession, ever watchful, ever prepared. He saw the spikes of the large iron gate that rose above his head and shivered. If it fell, they would all be killed under the crushing weight.

Another gatehouse was positioned a mere forty feet away with more guards stationed there. The parallel stone arches supported a room directly above the drawbridge where a heavy timber grille could be lowered. Intruders could be caught between them and shot with arrows from the slits in the walls of the towers. Jude imagined it a horrible way to die, being picked off in a small confined space. As they passed through the second gatehouse, now back on solid ground, off the drawbridge, Jude was relieved. He had felt claustrophobic and nervous as they rode through. Glancing over at Drelindah, watching her slight shiver, he knew he had not been alone in his feelings.

"How do the men gain entrance to the towers?" Jude asked Winian about the large defensive structures.

"The towers in the outer wall have staircases located against their inner face while the towers on the inner wall have twisting staircases built into the walls of each tower." Winian explained.

Jude listened intently, fascinated with the size and grandeur of Crispin Ebudai's home.

The walls were all perfectly vertical except along the bottom of the outer face where they spread out at a sharp angle making a sloping base. The towers could each be sealed off and defended independently of the rest of the wall in case of attack. Wooden planks located at wall-walk level behind each tower were the only way of getting from one section to another. Of the towers themselves there were two ways to get in. The first was at the base that opened up into the bottom room. Each tower had three small rooms, one on top of the other connected by a spiral staircase built into the stone. The second entrance was at the turret that could only be reached by the wall-walk.

A set of twenty foot high iron doors now confronted the procession and just as Jude was about to ask Winian what they had to do to get beyond this point, the heavy doors reinforced with iron straps swung slowly open. This final entryway could be braced from behind with a drawbar. Again as Jude looked up, he saw guards staring down at them, ever vigilant.

Riding under the last of the gatehouses, Jude was amazed at the sight now in front of him. The inner ward, stone on all sides, sparkled with the glow of thousands of lanterns. The walls were draped in brocade and silks; a carpet of red cloth was laid out for the procession and flower petals rained from high above them thrown from the hands of hundreds of the lairds' followers standing side-by-side along the battlements. Crispin Ebudai himself stood on a raised dais covered in red gharma blossoms and ivy.

Winian watched Jude's eyes sparkle with joy, saw him catch some of the petals in his hand, and noticed those that clung to the dark curls. It was physically painful for him to think of Jude being claimed by his mate, a mindless brute. He had to speak to Crispin immediately about making a claim of his own. In the enormous courtyard, the procession stopped, and Winian saw his brother Jaan Anek appear at the top of the hill that overlooked the lower bailey. And while he was overjoyed to see his brother, it was tempered with anger as his eyes washed over the men who so obviously belonged to the baroness. Guardians were enormous men, and it was easy to spot them.

Winian tried to keep his attention on Drelindah and Crispin, wanting to know, as did everyone, what her reception of the man would be. But instead he moved sideways as he dismounted and grabbed hold of Jude's arm, keeping him there at his side, not letting him bolt up the hill toward his mate even though he had no idea to which one of the giants Jude belonged.

The first thing Eoin noticed was the light that came into Jude's eyes when he saw him. It was a wholly satisfying experience. The way the brown eyes heated and darkened, the wicked smile and the way his chest tightened, it pleased Eoin to no end. The man could not deny that he had missed him; it was etched in every part of him.

When he saw Jude move to fly to him, it was then he noticed the man to Jude's left, holding him, restraining him, keeping him close. Only the hand of his fenris on his shoulder kept Eoin from drawing his broadsword and charging down the hill to slaughter the man who dared to put a hand on his mate.

Eoin Thral swallowed hard so he wouldn't roar out his anger. How dare anyone stand between a guardian and his mate? The bond was sacred. Didn't the man know that Jude Shea was the one soul in all of existence born to be his? Didn't he know that there would only ever be Jude? Didn't he know that Eoin would never, ever, allow anyone else to have his mate? Jude was his, only his, and though every part of him demanded he eviscerate the man walking with his mate and Drelindah up the hill, Eoin reined in the overwhelming urge and remained frozen.

Time slowed. Jude was aware of everything: the chilled morning breeze, the flutter of silk in the dirt as Drelindah's gown skated over the ground, and the breath he was holding in instead of breathing out. As Drelindah reached Crispin Ebudai, he bowed low before holding out his hand. When without hesitation she slipped hers into his, the crowd went wild at the same time as the sky was suddenly filled with flying arrows.

Screams and shouting filled the air as soldiers raced to the drawbridge to raise it and keep the marauders out. Winian didn't recover from the shock in time to keep hold of Jude's arm when everyone started running for shelter and safety. People scurried from the courtyard in droves, and as he lost sight of Jude in the surging crowd. He had no choice but to retreat toward the keep.

Eoin never lost sight of his mate. Nothing distracted him, not fear for his own life in the hail of arrows, not the surprise that the holding was under attack, and not the chaos of the fleeing crowd. So instead of losing Jude as Winian had, he bolted around the side of the keep where he had seen Jude pull several children and their mothers to safety.

Jude was herding people toward the stables and running back and forth looking for more when he was suddenly grabbed and yanked up against the side of the keep. The impact was hard and winded him for a moment before he looked up to yell at his assailant. And then he couldn't breathe for an altogether different reason.

"What in the name of the five gods are you about, Jude Shea?" Eoin roared at him, enraged that Jude was taking the chance of being hurt or killed. His hands were on his mate's face, looking him over, checking to make sure Jude wasn't hurt. "Are you mad?"

Jude felt the emotion rising out of him as he looked up into the dark pools of his lover's eyes. Had he ever been happier to see anyone in his whole life?

Eoin noted the trembling. "Were you scared?"

Jude hadn't been scared for a second. He was much too busy saving people to be scared. The tears that welled up in his eyes and blurred his vision had nothing to do with fear and everything to do with the man standing in front of him.

"Are you hurt, *cairn?*"

Heart.

Cairn meant *heart* and love and mate and everything all rolled up together. He couldn't speak and so simply brushed Eoin's hands off his face and lunged at him.

The smile through the tears, the soft eyes, the way he was needed... it was all too much for Eoin. He wrapped Jude up in his arms, crushing him against his big, hard body as their lips met in a frenzy of wanting. The kiss was hot and devouring, Eoin's tongue invading Jude's mouth, staking his claim as the man in his arms wrapped his long legs around Eoin's hips, squeezing tight. When he broke the kiss, unable to go without air a second more, he was faced with a panting, swollen-lipped, narrow-eyed Jude. The man simply annihilated him.

"I—"

"I love you." Jude tightened his arms around Eoin's neck, his legs around his hips. "I should have told you before you left, but I didn't because I thought it was too soon."

"Jude—"

"I was terrified to trust again, but I have to because I love you."

"Jude—"

"I'm so great at work, ya know," Jude plowed on, not even noticing Eoin's trembling lower lip, the desperate need in his eyes, or the way his mouth had been open to speak. "I've got all the confidence in the world when it comes to what I do, to my job, but in relationships... and my last one just... and so because of all that... because of things you had nothing to do with, I let you leave without telling you how I feel, but when I was in the river saving Winian's life and before that when—"

"Of what river do you speak, *cairn?*"

"Just—that doesn't matter. Only you matter." Jude's voice was raspy and filled with gravel. "I love you, so please, just stay with me, all right? Just stay."

Eoin stared into the brown eyes he loved more than anything. "You love me, then?"

"Yes, I do."

He loved him. Eoin let the words sink into his soul. Never had he been loved before; only Jude had ever seen within him anything worth having or claiming or keeping. Only his mate saw in him a man worth loving who could love in return. Eoin had to clear his throat and swallow the lump there before he could speak.

"I love you as well, Jude Shea. You are my own."

Jude leaned forward to kiss his mate, but Drist was suddenly there, his arm flying between them.

"Maul your mate in your bed," the Fenris of Saraso barked at Eoin. "We must get to the wall and stand with Crispin and Drelindah. Send Jude away."

But there was not a chance that Eoin was leaving Jude's side, even for a moment. Duty stood behind love; there was no other way for it to be.

Jude's life, in his opinion, was back to looking like a big summer blockbuster. All he was missing was Orlando Bloom. The archers lined up on the wall, the men with spears and swords behind them, and in the courtyard below, more men swords and maces. Everyone was in armor except for the guardians, and Jude thought that Eoin should get some on. He said as much as he was being dragged up stairs built into the walls and along the battlements. When he finally stood close to Drelindah, he saw the mid-morning light glittering off what looked like thousands of armored knights below him. They were surrounded.

As Jude listened he realized that the man doing the talking from outside the wall was Prefect Lyan Han, leader of the king's army. He had come to save Drelindah, as the king was most concerned about her safety. The fact that Lyan was there, having had to move so many men in so short a time was what had Crispin Ebudai perplexed. How did the king know the baroness had been kidnapped before the event even occurred? Any lingering doubts Drelindah had disappeared at that moment.

The king was trying to kill her; only the Bishop had interceded and saved her life. Had she reached the royal palace at Goren, she would have been tried and executed. There was no choice left to her; her new path was to walk beside Crispin Ebudai and prepare for war. When she stepped forward and delivered her words to the king's prefect, there was no hesitancy in her words. She ordered his troops off Crispin's land that now extended to Saraso. She and Crispin Ebudai were united. When Crispin stepped forward beside Drelindah and told the prefect that he and the Baroness of Saraso were to be married that very night, there was cheering from the battlements and from the courtyard below.

"I...." Drelindah gasped, ready to argue, but she could say nothing more as Crispin grabbed her and kissed her breathless.

The clapping from below from the king's troops, begun by Lyan Han, was unexpected.

"You make a mockery of my love for this woman?" Crispin growled down at the prefect.

Jude elbowed Drelindah in the arm, and her head swiveled to look at him. No one but the man from the other side of the veil would dare to touch her.

"Love," Jude mouthed the word to her, tipping his head at Crispin. "He loves you."

She flushed beet red and widened her eyes at him. "You are a horrible man!" she mouthed the words back silently.

He waggled his eyebrows at her, and she startled everyone when she launched herself at him. It made the prefect smile as he lifted his hand.

"Truly I mock you not, laird, for I see that you care for the lady. Our mission was to return her, but as we cannot, we will return to Goren and await your coming. There are barons with you and some with us… we will see who will claim the throne when this action is ended."

There was a flurry of activity as soon as Lyan Han gave the order to withdraw. He was a smart man; the holding built into the side of the mountain could not be taken, and by riding away, he had saved his men. He was unsure of how long their deaths would be averted; from the reports of the size of Crispin Ebudai's army, as well as the amount of men Drelindah Holt had at her disposal, along with the other barons who would surely join them, it was only a matter of time before the king would be overthrown and forced into exile. For now, he would march his men back the way they had come, which would take a month as he could not move his men through the pass that the Baroness of Saraso held.

Drelindah Holt sent Drist and Arius back down the mountain to Saraso immediately. She wanted to be certain that her holding was guarded, and she wanted to let Greshan Kai know that she was safe. She had not seen him since she had been kidnapped by Winian Anek.

"Drelindah," Crispin said as they crossed the courtyard together, her hand in his, "Illyrian Tor, my second, will ride with Arius and Drist. He will take men with him to protect Saraso as well."

Jude watched Drelindah's eyes fill, and when she looked at him, he made the *aww* face for her.

"I will have you beaten," she threatened as she smiled through her tears, rushing to keep up with the long strides of the man she was to marry.

Jude was so busy teasing the baroness that he didn't see Winian move up beside him. So when he was wrenched from Eoin's grip on his hand, he was surprised.

"What are you doing?" Jude asked Winian as the man faced him.

"I will speak to Crispin about—"

"How dare you touch my mate!" Eoin thundered at the man as he hurled him to the ground, stepping in front of Jude. "You will die for this trespass!"

Even before Winian could roll to his feet, Crispin was there between the two men. "Speak to me the importance of this man that he is the cause of strife."

"This is Jude Shea from through the veil," Eoin told Crispin, "and he is my mate."

Crispin looked at Winian Anek. "The veil is a myth, brother Anek, but the guardian claims the man as his mate." He looked at Jude. "Is this so? Are you the guardian's mate?"

"I am," Jude told him.

He was going to say something when he noticed Jude's eyes. They were brown, and Crispin Ebudai had never seen such a color. "Then be at peace, brother Anek," Crispin soothed Winian, "for you will have many to choose from, and the guardian has but one."

The reasoning did nothing to soothe Winian's hackled pride. "As you say, laird," he said, taking a step back.

Eoin grabbed Jude's bicep, nearly wrenching the smaller man's arm off as he marched him up the hill toward the keep.

"Stop," Jude said softly, his fingers on Eoin's hand.

"Why would the man presume to speak for you, Jude Shea? What did you promise or invite that he would—"

"What?" Jude was stunned. "What'd you say?"

"Perhaps my absence had to be filled with—"

"Oh fuck you," Jude yelled, planting his left foot, bending at the knee and then sweeping his right leg out.

Eoin's momentum carried him forward a second before Jude's movement jerked him backward and then down. Flat on his back staring up at his mate, he was dumbfounded.

"I know you don't know me that well, but I would—"

"Jude."

"I am loyal, and—"

"What have you done?" Eoin cut off his rant.

"What?"

Eoin gestured around. "How did you put me on my back, Jude Shea?"

Jude scowled down at his mate. "Don't try and change the subject. You just accused me of—"

The guardian sat up in the dirt, still staring up at his mate. "You have been trained to defend yourself, *cairn*?"

"I live in Chicago," Jude snapped at the ignorant man at his feet. "Of course I can defend myself. You think I'd last five seconds if I couldn't?"

Eoin knew Jude was mad; the flushed skin, flashing eyes, and hands balled into fists all told him as much, but he could not stop smiling to save his life. The man was a vision, and Jude belonged to him.

"What the hell's wrong with you?" Jude yelled at him again. How could Eoin ever think that Jude would even look at another man as long as they were together? Jude was in love with him! Didn't that mean *anything*?

Eoin rose slowly until he was once more towering over Jude, looking down at the man who never ceased to amaze him. Jude was fragile and delicate but had put down a guardian with so fluid a movement that Eoin didn't even have time to counter.

"If you think I would ever—"

Eoin fisted his hand in Jude's hair and yanked his head backward before he sealed his mouth over the smaller man's and kissed him hungrily. Jude's righteous indignation, the fire in his eyes, all of it told Eoin what he needed to know. His mate had done nothing to purposely ensnare Winian Anek's interest, for Jude cared only for him.

Jude wrapped his arms around Eoin's neck and lifted himself up, kissing the man back with all the pent-up emotion from the last few days. He wanted to go home; he wanted to take Eoin with him, because he was ready for his life to start with Eoin at his side.

"Where is your room?" Jude asked his mate, pulling back to whisper in his ear, his breath warm and wet.

Eoin knew he needed to go to the baroness; he needed to thank Crispin Ebudai for interceding so he didn't have to kill Winian Anek; and he needed to see Drist before the man left, but all his duty, again, paled beside the allure of his mate. Eoin needed Jude, and until his desire was sated, he was useless to any but the man in his arms.

"Eoin," Jude moaned, "please."

Instead of carrying him, Eoin took Jude's hand in his and led him from the courtyard around the back of the keep to the enormous kitchen. Through the buttery there were winding stairs that led up to the second floor, and down a long dark hallway, there was a small door that Eoin had to duck under. Inside the tiny room was only a bed. It was all Jude needed.

He heard the bolt slide into place behind him, and when Jude turned to face his massive lover; he saw the hunger there in Eoin's eyes. Jude was thankful for the small window, because even though the sky outside was dark and grey, the light was still enough that he could watch as the man stripped out of his clothes and revealed slowly the heavily muscled frame, the hard chiseled chest, and the deep groove that ran down his abdomen to the flat stomach. His eyes slid lower as Eoin's pants slipped from his narrow hips to free the huge, uncircumcised cock that was stiff and ready for him. Jude had never seen an uncut penis before Eoin but found the thick, prominent veins and dark foreskin very sexy. He now knew from experience that the length and girth had filled and stuffed him as he had never been, and he wanted to be again. As he wet his lips, Jude stepped closer and reached for the long, hard shaft, his fingers brushing over the flared head.

"You haven't let me suck you," Jude said, lowering himself to his knees, his hand sliding down Eoin's throbbing cock to the thick base. "How come?"

His mouth dry, his eyes riveted to Jude's pale pink lips, Eoin tried to get words out. "The women spoke that I… I am big and ugly and to… oh…." The groan was torn from his soul as Jude's mouth closed over him, taking in as much as he could without gagging. "Jude," he gasped, his hands fisted in his mate's hair as sensations he had never thought to know swept through him.

Jude's throat opened up, and he took Eoin all the way down, then back and down again. It was not an action to be repeated, the man was simply too big. Jude fisted the shaft, sucking and licking, bathing the engorged length of his lover in saliva; his hands stroking and squeezing the now sensitized cock. His tongue slid under the foreskin along the length and into the slit at the end, and then he swirled his tongue around the enormous head before swallowing what he could of the man. He sucked so hard, the suction so strong and good, that Eoin knew his control was soon to shatter.

"Stop," Eoin whimpered, unable to move, afraid that if he came Jude would be repulsed, afraid to move in case his mate stopped.

Jude increased his tempo, his pressure, used his hands to gently squeeze and caress, every touch meant to drive his lover wild. His mouth moved to the heavy balls, laving, sucking before turning his attention back to the rock-hard shaft as he fondled what wouldn't fit into his mouth and throat. Jude knew that he was making the man crazy with his ministrations, as evidenced by Eoin's rasping breath and the way he was pumping in and out of his mouth, increasing his rhythm with each stroke, unable to stop. The motion so primal, so deeply engrained, that Eoin could only anchor Jude still as he fucked his mouth.

"Jude!" Eoin roared, and it was loud in the small room.

His throat suddenly filled, Jude swallowed the hot cum that seemed endless, drank it all down, and then held his lover between his lips and licked him clean. Eoin watched in breathless wonder, never taking his eyes off his lover. The ecstasy, raw and powerful, had drained him as surely as the man had.

"So," Jude said, rising to his feet in front of his lover, taking hold of the flaccid penis, "I never want to hear that any part of you is not hot or sexy or beautiful because I love every piece of you, Eoin Thral, and this part is especially important to me. In fact, it's mine."

His words combined with his actions sent Eoin into a frenzy of motion. He would devour Jude Shea body and soul; there was no other way for it to be. Shoving Jude down hard on the bed, Eoin came down on top of him, pinning the smaller man in place.

"Oh yeah." Jude wiggled under Eoin's muscular frame, his legs wrapping around his lover's hips. "You want me."

The feeling was so much darker and harder and more desperate than want. Eoin's heart wanted to burst from his chest; it was almost unbearable, the feelings coursing through him, the carnal heat and the craving to taste his mate.

"Eoin," Jude sighed the man's name. "I love you."

Eoin bit down hard, his jaw clenching as he shivered with the primitive need to both bed and devour his love. For the first guardians had drunk the blood of their mates to keep them strong, and the ancestral thirst now roared through his veins. There was a throbbing desire to consume Jude, to keep him with him always, to hide him away from everyone else.

"Kiss me." Jude smiled up at Eoin, stretching languidly under him, never sensing his jeopardy. If Eoin didn't bury himself inside Jude in seconds, he would go mad. He hoped that the surging, driving feelings would soothe with time, because to have the desire stay peaked forever would mean that Jude Shea would need to be chained to his bed.

The rumbling groan that came from his lover made Jude catch his breath. He enjoyed knowing that he drove the man wild.

Eoin could not think about Jude tied up and begging. The thought did nothing to calm his raging desire. As he ground his mouth down over his mate's, he felt Jude melt beneath him, sink into the bed, into the ravishment. Eoin moaned into his mate's mouth before he wrenched free, lifting up to untangle the man from him, his arms and his legs, so that he could tear Jude from his clothes to reach his skin.

"I missed you," Jude whispered under him, and Eoin was undone.

He wished he were a courtier at that moment, a man who could use words and write them artfully, because he wanted to express the depth of his love, how full his heart was, how close to bursting. But he was a soldier, and worse, a beast. Eoin was a man who spoke seldom, and there was no forum but strength for him to exhibit the feelings roaring through him. He had no voice to speak his soul; there was only action.

Jude found himself flipped over on his stomach and then lifted roughly to his hands and knees. Before he could even look over his shoulder at his rapacious lover, he felt his ass cheeks spread before Eoin's long wet tongue rimmed his opening.

"Oh God," Jude gasped, his hands fisting in the blankets as he pushed back onto the thick muscle sliding deeper and deeper into his quickly loosening hole.

Eoin's hands dug into his slender hips as he licked and sucked and nibbled Jude's ass until the smaller man was trembling under him, shouting for Eoin to stop screwing around and fuck him already.

"Speak again," Eoin teased him, somehow finding that as Jude's desire rose to a fever pitch, his own calmed. Knowing that Jude wanted him, craved him, and needed him, gave Eoin Thral peace.

"Fuck me!"

Oh, how Eoin loved that filthy word! Coming from Jude, who was so beautiful and elegant and perfect... to hear Jude scream to be taken made him instantly hard as a rock. Was there a sweeter sound than Jude's whimper of need?

He was wet, ready, and writhing under Eoin, so when he lifted Jude's hips slightly and plunged down into him to the hilt, he knew that the gasp that came from his lover was pure pleasure and not pain. When Eoin entered him, the enormous penis filling him, stuffing him full, Jude thought he was going to explode right there. But it was the slow withdrawal and then the powerful second lunge that did it. Eoin rubbed over his prostate, hitting it each time he moved in and out of him, and the pressure and the stroking built so fast, Jude was drowning under a wave of sensation before he even knew he was lost. He screamed Eoin's name as he came, semen splashing on the sheet beneath him.

Watching his enormous swollen rod slide in and out of his mate's firm round ass was almost more that Eoin could bear. That his mate could take in his entire length, shudder in pleasure, and beg him not to stop pushed Eoin over the edge. His strokes became a pounding, driving, plunging rhythm as he pushed Jude forward across the bed until he hit the wall. Anchoring his hands above his mate's head, Eoin used the stone under his hands as leverage and slammed into his mate. He never wanted to stop. The muscles in Jude's ass contorted around him, holding him tight as he threw back his head and shouted Jude's name.

He collapsed on top of his mate, and Jude buckled under Eoin as he was crushed down onto the bed. Sweating, semen coating his thighs, panting hard, Jude could not remember ever being so sated, loved so hard and so well. When Eoin lifted up off him, he rolled over to his back and pulled Jude into his arms. Jude couldn't even help, momentarily exhausted from their coupling.

"We have a problem, and we have to talk about it."

Eoin nuzzled his face into Jude's hair and pressed him tighter to him. All he had thought about for a week was Jude molded to his side, and now he finally had the man where he wanted him.

"I can't go home."

Eoin leaned back to look at his lover. "You will and you must, love."

"And will you be coming with me?"

The guardian knew he was caught and so forced a smile for his mate. "I will join you as soon as I am able."

Before Jude could get worked up, before he could even get out a word, Eoin leaned in and kissed him. When he slid his tongue across the seam of Jude's lips, they were parted instantly as Eoin rolled Jude over on his back.

"Love." Eoin smiled down at his mate, brushing the hair back from his face. "I cannot leave the baroness now with the king's men at her door; I owe her more service for her shelter and feeding of me."

"You're not her pet; you're a man and she might have given you a home but you've protected her with your life and now that life belongs to me. That's what you told me."

"'Tis the truth."

"Well then you need to come home with me."

"I cannot leave the baroness or my brethren when I am needed."

"I need you."

"Aye but well you—"

"Fine then I'll stay here until—"

"You cannot stay," Eoin told him, and his conviction was absolute. "Well you know this."

"I won't leave you."

"Aye, love, you will."

"I won't," Jude assured him.

Eoin spread Jude's legs and settled himself between his mate's thighs. "You will do as I say, *cairn*, for I cannot hope to offer my baroness my heart or my sword if both are guarding you. How will I grant her aid if I cannot leave your side?"

"You said you would come home with me," Jude reminded him. "You swore you would, and now you're what... taking it back?"

Eoin needed to make Jude understand, but it was difficult, as the younger man was not a soldier. There was no possible way that he could return with Jude, knowing that the other men he had fought alongside of for years could lose their lives due to his absence. He could never desert his comrades; there was no honor in that.

"You promised me—"

"All has changed, *cairn*, and you and I both must as well. The river does not rage at the rocks but simply changes course as need be."

"Yeah, that's great, really Zen, but here's the thing... if you stay here, so do I."

"I will not allow such."

"I don't care," Jude asserted. "I won't leave here without you."

"You will!"

Jude felt rather than heard Eoin's words. "We can do this all night."

"I cannot have you here, love," Eoin said, his voice low and husky, "my heart... I need to know you are safe and that my home is with you and waiting for my return."

"No," Jude argued, the tears welling up in his eyes because he was frustrated. "I won't leave—"

Eoin bent and cut off Jude's words with a kiss, sucking the plump bottom lip inside his hot mouth before nibbling it gently.

Jude wrapped his legs around his mate's hips, wanting to hold the man close to him.

"Love," Eoin breathed into his mouth before pulling back so he could see Jude's beautiful eyes. "I need you to hear me. Torn in half serves none; you need to return to your home, be safe there, and make certain that there is a place for me."

Jude had just found the man, discovered that he loved him, and now he was supposed to walk away? Was he high? "You are seriously on something if you think I can just leave here and not know if you're alive or… If I'm here, I can see you and watch your back and—"

"But this serves only you," Eoin interrupted him.

"I don't care."

Eoin smiled at the defiant tone, the clenched jaw, and the glare he was receiving. "Alas, I do, *cairn*. To wake each day and know you are safe, this then will bring me comfort."

"And so what, on my end I just get to wonder if you're alive or dead?" Jude's voice rose as he tried to get Eoin off of him, shoving at the rock-hard chest.

"Aye, love, 'tis the place of the mate," Eoin answered solemnly. "You must wait, tending to hearth and home, for my return."

"No," Jude yelled at him, twisting and turning, squirming out from under Eoin, moving before the big man could stop him.

Watching Jude pace naked back and forth beside the bed made Eoin's heart swell with love for the man; at the same time, looking at his flushed skin, glittering eyes, and lean but defined muscles was pure pleasure. He was ready to argue and debate, and Eoin knew that Jude was prepared to pound him into submission, no matter how long it took.

"Are you listening to me?"

The guardian had been concentrating on the play of muscles in his mate's back, on the indentations in each ass cheek, on the way his hair fell across his collarbone, and how he was nervously biting the lower lip. That drove the guardian crazy. It was all Eoin could do to not grab the man and wrap him in his arms.

"Eoin?"

"Oh aye, love," he answered quickly, "I heard you."

Jude knew when he was being placated. "Oh yeah? What'd I say?"

"You spoke that you will remain here with me."

"Yes," Jude said.

"No." Eoin shook his head, and before Jude could start another rant, he grabbed his hand and yanked hard. Jude ended up in his arms, in his lap, with Eoin hugging him tight.

Jude wanted to push away, but he found himself clutching Eoin back, his face buried in the side of the guardian's neck, holding on for dear life.

Eoin was certain that if the roles were reversed, he would be just as traumatized as his mate was. To have to live with the uncertainty of the other's safety, not knowing his fate, this would be maddening. He wished he could give the younger man solace, but allowing Jude to remain in Midrin was not an option. Jude needed to be safe.

"I wish I didn't love you."

Eoin stroked the soft hair as the arms and legs around him tightened. And even though Jude couldn't see the smile, he heard it in the man's voice. "You cannot take back your heart, _cairn_. You gifted me with that treasure."

But his heart was breaking, and Jude knew in that moment that he had not been in love before. It had never felt like this, never hurt as much, never felt like there was a cold wind blowing through him, like there was a gaping hole in his chest.

"Please don't send me away," Jude begged softly, his voice barely able to get out around the lump in his throat.

"Jude—"

"I'll stop loving you."

"You cannot stop now that you have begun."

"If you send me away, you should just stay here and forget about me."

Eoin's snort of laughter triggered Jude's tears. "You will not lose me, Jude Shea. Well I know that my life belongs to you. I would not be gone from your side and allow another into your heart. Never will there be other than me."

Jude wanted to crawl inside the man's skin, be part of him, be closer. And as the hand slid down the slope of his spine to the small of his back, Jude felt his cock stir. "I want you inside me... please, Eoin."

There had been heat before, and raging passion and desperate need, but until then there had not been the slow, sensual joining. Eoin felt as though he had been hurled into the sun. The intensity of Jude's gaze, how hot his body was inside, and the marks his mate left on him—all of it meant to be branded on his soul. As though he could forget the feel of his mate's skin, the taste of his lips, his musky scent, or the tight channel that held and milked the length of him! Jude's legs draped over his shoulders, the man's back bowed, his head thrown back in ecstasy, all of it was forever imprinted on Eoin's memory, never to be erased or forgotten. The brown eyes locked on his, dark liquid pools full of absolute, unconditional love.

As they lay together later, utterly spent, it was Eoin who lifted up off bed, pulled the engraved silver band off his middle finger, and slid it onto the thumb of Jude's left hand.

"You find a chain when you return home. The ring marks me as a guardian, and as I have no time to have one made for you. It is yours until I bring you your own, *cairn*."

Jude ran his fingers across the runes. "It says guardian?"

"It is my name and the word guardian."

"Well, since I'm the guardian of your heart, I'll take good care of it."

Eoin nodded, pulling Jude into his arms, holding him against his heart. "You are my guardian, Jude Shea... forget me not."

But there was no chance of that ever happening; Eoin Thral didn't need to worry.

Chapter Ten

DRELINDAH HOLT was stunned at the enormity of her guardian's sacrifice, and while she was touched down to her soul, the guilt was overwhelming as well. Already she saw the change in Eoin Thral. As he delivered his decision to her at the evening meal, she saw hardness in his eyes, a deadening of spirit that was painful to see. He kept his mate tucked against his side, spoke to no one but Jude, and dipped his head often to listen to the smaller man. Eoin had been amazed when he learned how exactly Jude had saved Winian Anek, and his eyes had glowed briefly with pride. But he couldn't hold onto his happiness, the weight of being parted from Jude too heavy, too painful not to crush him. Drelindah's heart hurt watching Jude as well, seeing the pain build until the smaller man just leaned into Eoin. When the door was suddenly thrown open, she was happy for the intrusion.

Jude was so lost in his own misery that he didn't realize he was getting yanked to his feet until Eoin was barking orders at him.

"What's wrong?" he asked as he was being dragged from the hall.

"The king's men did not withdraw, and we are under attack. They scale the walls even now."

"But that man, Lyan Han, the prefect… he said that—"

"He was killed by his second-in-command, branded a traitor and coward, and now his troops attack us as they were ordered to do by the king."

Jude breathed an enormous sigh of relief. "Then I can just stay with—"

"No," Eoin cut him off, pulling him along after him. "You leave now for the veil. We are closer than you know. You will run where I show you, and when you clear the mist you will be home."

"I hafta go now?" Jude nearly choked, flushed with terror.

"Aye," Eoin said absently, looking around fast, following the stream of men to the kitchen and outside. The dark sky was full of flaming arrows; people were running from all sides, the smell of smoke filled the air, the sound of ringing steel, screams and shouting.

"Wait," Jude planted his feet. "I'm not ready to—"

"There is no time," Eoin cut him off, grabbing his arms, shaking him hard. "You have no time to delay, *cairn*, you have to run and not look back."

"But how will I know if you're okay?"

Eoin didn't answer; he just yanked Jude off his feet and ran. Jude had to run or fall and be dragged after the guardian. It was terrifying; the men who fell wounded and dying in front of him, even more so that leaving Eoin was imminent.

He needed more time. There was a rendezvous to be arranged, a timetable to be agreed upon, a backup plan to be made and promises to be sworn. Jude had more to say and more to do, and most of all he wanted to be back in bed with Eoin warm and naked under him. He wasn't ready to leave.

"Wait," Jude tried to yell over the din of battle, but it was useless. Eoin was completely focused on getting him out of the keep, nothing else.

Eoin ran toward the stable, barreling through several men barring his path, and continued down toward the main gate. At the last moment, he veered left, and Jude saw the men fighting along the wall. He didn't realize that Eoin was armed until he saw the man coming toward him and saw the enormous broadsword that his mate brandished to ward off the attack. And as Eoin fought the man and kept Jude at his back, he understood the nightmare that his mate was living through. He had to defend himself and protect Jude all at the same time. It was too much to ask of anyone.

When the attacker was struck down, Jude was jerked forward, and he and Eoin made it to the opening in the wall before they were faced with more of the king's soldiers.

"Guardian! Come here to me!"

Eoin saw Winian Anek motioning to him and without thought ran to the man. Whatever their differences, whatever Winian's desire was for Jude, they were brothers-in-arms the moment the attack had begun.

"Are you out for an evening stroll?" he teased Eoin, passing him an enormous tower shield from one of his fallen men.

"Aye," Eoin breathed out, gripping the shield, holding it around Jude before locking his eyes with those of his mate. "Winian and I will hold here, but you must run, Jude Shea, and do not look back… run as you never have."

Jude was panicked, his hands reaching out to grip Eoin's heavily padded vest over the linen shirt he wore. "Come with me."

"I cannot, well you know this," he almost yelled at his mate, terrified that at any moment they would be overrun and Jude would be killed before his eyes. "Run down the hill and stop for no one! Run now!"

But even when Eoin shoved him away, Jude didn't move... he couldn't. And part of him knew he was being the character in the movie that everybody yells at, the one the hero sacrifices everything for and ends up getting killed, but he was powerless to leave the man he loved. The pull to stay, the need to stay, was overwhelming.

"Jude!" Eoin roared at him. "Run!"

"Jude, you will be the death of us!" Winian yelled at him.

But he was rooted to the spot.

Eoin knew his mate was overwrought; it was stamped on the man, in his haunted eyes, his trembling breath, the white-knuckled hands holding onto him. There was nothing to be done; Jude was incapable of simply running away from him. With a frustrated growl, Eoin moved the shield, shoved the sword at Winian, and fisted his hand in Jude's shirt, wrenching him forward against him. The kiss he delivered was rough and deep, bruising and fast, and Eoin bit down hard so Jude would have the blood to taste as he ran. He knew his mate needed a long goodbye, but there was no time. It was all he could give him. As Jude looked up at his mate, he saw Eoin's head lift, his eyes beyond him.

"Run!" Winian shouted as he tossed Eoin the sword.

Plucking the flying weapon from the air, Eoin's fingers tightened on the hilt as he turned and swung. By the time the killing stroke was completed, Jude was flying across the field away from his mate, having finally done as he was ordered. It was too much to ask, though, that Jude did not look back. At the edge of the forest, he stopped and turned. Jude spied Eoin once before he saw the men on horseback start after him across the field. They had their swords drawn; they were riding hard, obviously on their way to kill him. Turning away fast, Jude plunged into the tree line.

The sounds of battle faded as Jude ran deeper into the forest. It was dark, and he lost his footing several times but never fell. The branches from the trees whipped at him, scratched him, ripping and tearing as he ran on and on. He worried when the fog thickened that he was going to run into a tree and knock himself out or worse, but then he remembered that the mist was hiding him, and that was comforting. It wasn't scary; it was the veil, and that meant home.

When he slid forward, his boot catching on something, he went flying only to wind up tumbling into a large muddy puddle. Sitting up, dripping water, he saw the sprinkler head he had tripped over. As the fog slowly cleared, he saw the swing set, the streetlight beyond it, and the Lexus driving at a crawl through the empty intersection. He was back on his street, but instead of elation, there was only the crushing weight of despair. Nothing could be or would be right without Eoin Thral. What the hell was he going to do?

Chapter Eleven

EVERYONE was worried, but no one had to be. He was fine. Everything was fine. Jude must have repeated those words ten times, twenty times a day, to everyone who called or sent him an e-mail or popped into his office. He had scared his family, friends, co-workers—everyone—with his little disappearing act. They all wanted answers, but there was only one person who could know and accept the truth.

Jude's older brother, Ben, the person he trusted more than anyone on the planet, the person who always *listened*... Ben got the truth. Only Ben heard about the veil and Midrin and Eoin Thral. And because he was Ben, because he always accepted and never questioned and never doubted, Jude was able to unburden his heart.

His brother asked lots of questions and categorized the answers for future use, because Benjamin Shea, the deputy U.S. marshal, the man who put people into witness protection, he was the one who would create Eoin's new identity when the time came. Jude understood then that really, truly, everything happened for a reason. Even Ben's choice of a career had a reason behind it that would now benefit Jude when the time came. He would never believe in coincidence again. His brother was a blessing, as was his lovely new boss.

When Jude had called Natalie Torres the following day after his return, apologizing for not being in New York when they had agreed, she had chuckled and told him that he really needed to start listening. His self-imposed timetable had been fourteen days; her mandate had been a month. She wasn't expecting him. When he had not showed at the end of two weeks, she had been thrilled because she thought he was actually listening to her.

"Well, shit," he had groaned on the phone, which had sent her into peals of laughter. They were going to get along just fine. He had flown out to New York the following Monday.

Jude made his friend, Maya, stay at his apartment just in case Eoin showed up, but he really wasn't expecting the man. A war of the magnitude that Crispin Ebudai was waging on the kingdom of Goren would take months, maybe years to see to fruition. Jude had no idea when or if he would see the guardian again.

So as work sailed along, his professional life at a high point, he was miserable. During the day, when his mind was occupied and the demands on his time were overwhelming, he could push thoughts of Eoin Thral away. But at night, alone in his bed, it was torture. All he wanted was to be wrapped up in the arms of his demanding lover. It was harder than he thought to be without the love of his life after he found him.

He tried to connect with friends, but it was hard. It seemed like there should be guilt because he was sitting having fun, when a world away the love of his life was fighting for his. It seemed like it would be traitorous for Jude to be happy if Eoin was not there to share it with him. But Jude wanted a home for Eoin to join him in, and without friends, what kind of home would that be? He had to find a balance, and it came in the form of an unlikely source.

Colton Bale's father Quentin was on the board of directors of a new shelter/outpatient clinic they were building close to downtown. He came to his son to do some charity PR work for the new venture. Colton, who made a point of never mixing his business and personal life, asked Natalie to see if Jude would consider the task. Jude could barely understand his boss when she talked to him about it because she was laughing so hard.

"Is he kidding? He doesn't mix business and personal life? I'm sorry. Did he make that little mandate before or after he screwed your ex-boyfriend?"

Jude couldn't help smiling either. It was just too good. How hypocritical was that?

When Jude confronted Colton, Colton told him that he didn't want the project more because of his father's views on homosexuality than anything else. But Jude was certain that while Quentin Bale cared about *his* son being gay, Jude being gay would not be an issue. And he was right. Jude and the elder Bale got along famously.

The campaign for *My Brother's Keeper* was one of the best Jude ever designed, and the fundraising gala was a huge success. As a result of the wave of good press, new referrals, and flood of clients impressed with their community commitment and involvement, Sheridan Grant saw an opportunity. In the economic times that everyone faced, ethics in business was a focal point. Giving something back was just smart. Jude found himself promoted from creative director to community outreach director. No longer would he brainstorm big-budget campaigns for cutesy products and companies. Instead he would devote himself to marketing for the unseen and to make people aware of challenges and opportunities to make direct and impactful changes on their community. He was in charge of the charitable dollars at Sheridan Grant. It took almost every single drop of his time.

There were no nights out at clubs drinking and dancing; there were no parties and no weekend getaways. He had evenings at home with friends, saw movies with friends, and spent the remainder of his time, which was a very small amount, sleeping. He was busy, his life was passing in a blur, and he liked it. If he slowed down, he'd miss Eoin and the pain of the man's absence would eat him up. It was best the way things were. With six months of silence from his lover having already passed, there didn't seem to be an end in sight.

His friends noticed the change in Jude, a sort of sadness that clung to him. His beauty that had always been vibrant and alive was now dark and somber. He looked empty and haunted, and no one missed it, because it was both beautiful and painful to see. Jude, who had always been a man people noticed, was now one who it was hard to tear your eyes away from. Certainly Colton Bale could not.

Colton watched people watch Jude. He heard him get hit on, saw his complete obliviousness, and when someone made their intentions known, his utter disdain. Colton had not made that mistake. From the moment Jude had returned, Colton had been engaged in a campaign to make the man his friend. He had moved from coffee to lunches to dinners in Jude's office. He liked the rare occasions that Jude would laugh and he would see a glint in the brown depths of now hidden warmth. He liked that when they worked together, Jude would purposely now sit beside him, bring him coffee along with his, or pop into his office just to mention something instead of putting it in an e-mail. It was definite progress.

When they had a business retreat, Jude had suggested to the board that to save money, everyone should share rooms, from managing directors on down. It was novel, and when Colton asked Jude to be his roommate, he had been amazed that the younger man agreed. And while it was torture watching Jude in nothing but sweats, his tousled curls wet, grey sweatpants hanging off his narrow hips, the flat, cut abs, and sensual curve of his ass, Colton was thrilled to be trusted. When Jude fell asleep as they were watching TV, Colton looked his fill, taking in the defined chest, the pecs with the pink nipples, and all the smooth, olive skin. How he wanted to taste the man, drown in him and lose himself completely. The feelings were overwhelming, as was the regret that he had not begun his campaign the minute they had met instead of losing so much time.

Every day Jude let down another wall. Every day he laughed more, smiled more, let Colton in just a little more. If Colton had been smart enough to realize Jude was _the one_ six months ago, where would they be now? The fledgling closeness gave him hope, and when Jude agreed to have dinner with him when they got back, he could barely breathe. On his way down the hall toward Jude's office, he was floating on a cloud until he turned the corner and saw the man standing outside Jude's door.

"What are you doing here?" Colton barked at Tiernan Saunders, who had his hand on the door, fingers splayed out, gathering his courage to knock.

"I could ask you the same question," Tiernan snapped back at his ex-lover, intent on going in. "I need to talk to Jude, and since he won't take my—"

"Don't bother him just—"

"I asked what you're doing here," Tiernan rounded on Colton.

"I work here, you idiot."

"No." Tiernan's voice was icy. "I mean what are you doing here at Jude's door after work on a Friday night? That's my question."

"We're having dinner, if it's any of your business."

"Oh, fuck yeah, it's my business," Tiernan said as he pointed to the door. "My plan is to get that man back."

Colton snorted out his laughter. "Even I know that Jude's not the kind of guy to forget. You screwed him over so you're done."

"And you didn't? He's going to forgive you?"

"I—"

"What are you two doing?"

Both men turned to look at Jude's snarky assistant, Angel Vargas. She was a big, beautiful woman with an even bigger, louder personality. She guarded Jude with the ferocity of a mother hen with a touch of friendship thrown in for good measure. She had been his assistant the entire time he was with Sheridan Grant, and when he left, she had as well. Her husband could support her easily with his job as partner at one of the city's top law firms, but Angel liked to work, and even more so, she liked working for Jude Shea. She had returned with him the first day.

As Angel regarded the two men standing outside her boss's door, her brows instantly scrunched together. Tiernan Saunders had lost Jude and now wanted him back. Colton Bale just wanted, period. Neither one was good enough, in her opinion, which she would freely share if anyone asked.

"If you're looking for Jude, he is not here."

Both men looked surprised. *Oh, she was going to enjoy this.*

"Jude ran up out of here ten minutes ago when he got a call from home."

"His parents called him?" Tiernan asked, confused.

"No, honey, from his man."

Oh, that was fun, the looks on both men's faces.

"Jude doesn't—"

"He met someone when he was away on vacation, and his landlord called to ask if it was okay if he let the guy in to wait for him." She smiled evilly. "I had to answer for him, because my boss did not seem to be breathing at that moment. Apparently this man, Eoin something—I think he's Scottish," she threw in, "is Jude's man. I have never seen him move like that for anyone."

"But—"

"So goodnight, gentlemen." She beamed at them.

Colton Bale had to know; Tiernan was way ahead of him. Colton saw the elevator close as he started down the hall from Jude's office. That Tiernan was already on the elevator meant only one thing. The man had run.

THOUGHTS swirled through Jude's head as he sat in the cab headed for his apartment. Eoin was there. After six horrible, silent, barren months Eoin was there, at home, waiting for him. He leaned forward and asked the driver, again, to hurry.

He had found a perfect place for Eoin's studio, had gone ahead and leased it with the option to buy if his mate liked it when he saw it... if he saw it... no, *when*. It had been hard to stay positive, hard to remain hopeful when every day that went by made it harder to recall the man's scent, the sound of his voice, and the feel of his hands. Jude had never believed that grief could be physically painful, but he learned the hard way. But now the end to waiting was at hand, and Jude was terrified that he was going to wake up.

When the cab stopped, Jude shoved the two twenties at the man for the nine dollar cab ride and was gone before the driver could ask if he wanted change. Up three flights, Jude wasn't winded;

he was euphoric as he reached his front door. Throwing it open, he yelled Eoin's name even as an overwhelming sense of dread and fear descended on him. What if Eoin was there to tell him that he had to go back, or worse, knew that giving up being a guardian for Jude was a mistake, or *worse*, had fallen in love with someone else? What if Eoin didn't feel the same way? What if his heart no longer wanted Jude?

Jude felt his stomach heave as his voice disappeared. He could not have yelled again if he tried. Walking into the apartment, he realized that the small one-bedroom seemed suddenly cavernous as he moved through it. His heart was in his throat. But then....

There in Jude's bed, stretched out under the blanket, was Eoin Thral. Beside the bed in a pile were his clothes. He must have just stripped everything off, crawled under the blankets, and passed out. The long line of the muscular back was visible ,and from what Jude could see, it was both bruised and cut in several places. Closing on the bed slowly, careful not to wake his lover, Jude saw that his throat and face were bruised as well. Eoin had been in a terrible fight, and Jude had an almost overwhelming urge to call an ambulance. But he had no idea the amount of punishment a guardian's body could take, and Eoin was sleeping soundly. Taking a step back, he gasped as his wrist was grabbed tight, the fingers like steel that held him.

"Leave not my side."

Jude caught his breath as Eoin rolled over on his back and pulled the smaller man down on top of him. The second Jude was sprawled on top of him, he bent forward and kissed the guardian with every bit of longing and pain and desire that had been building up in him for half a year.

Eoin Thral felt the hot tears spilling from the corners of his eyes and rolling down into his ears. It was a dream, his best one, the one that kept him sane when there had been madness raging around him, the one that had anchored him while others were swept away into hopelessness and drowned in sorrow. He was with Jude, had Jude wrapped around him, and he could feel his mate's heart beating next to his. It was his favorite dream.

"Eoin Thral," Jude said breathlessly as he smiled and pulled back from the kiss that was not being returned. "If you expect to stay in my bed, you better kiss me back."

Eoin jolted under him, realizing only then that he was awake. Often he moved so quickly between dreams and consciousness that he couldn't separate them. But he was there, in Jude's bed, and it wasn't a dream. He had crossed through the veil, having been granted his freedom and sent to his mate.

"You're probably hungry." Jude cleared his throat, smiling tentatively, worried over the fact that Eoin had not returned his passion, concerned about the guardian's reaction—or lack thereof—to him. "I hafta go to the store, but I'll be right back."

Eoin watched Jude crawl off him.

"Don't leave all right?" he said softly before he turned and left the room.

He was gone. It took Eoin long minutes to process the interaction, and then he roared out his frustration. He was an idiot! Jude was unsure of him, and Eoin hated that. The man needed to hear and see and feel that he had been missed, had to know that Eoin had been lost without him and that all he wanted now was to be buried inside him. But instead of heat and desire, all Eoin had conveyed was hesitancy and uncertainty. What a stupid fool he was! He would have told Jude so, but the man was gone before Eoin could find his voice. It hurt to rise up from the bed, but it hurt more to be so close to Jude and not hold the man in his arms.

Jude was standing out on his front stoop, at an absolute loss. He could barely breathe. Eoin had not kissed him, had not held him, after six months apart… what did that say?

"Jude?"

Finding the voice, he saw Tiernan Saunders on the sidewalk looking up at him.

"Hey." Tiernan smiled at him, moving to the edge of the stairs as Jude slowly descended them.

"What are you doing here?"

"I went to your office, but—"

"Who told you where I lived?"

It was an odd question. "We still have friends in common, you know."

Jude nodded, shoving his hands in the pockets of his trench coat. "I guess."

"Is it all right if I talk to you?"

"We have nothing to talk about," Jude said turning away from Tiernan.

He stepped around in front of his ex-lover fast, barring Jude's path. "Where are you going? Maybe I could just walk with you."

Jude shrugged, too lost in thinking about Eoin to process anything else.

Tiernan breathed in a deep sigh of relief and would have started walking with Jude, but there was sudden sound of squealing tires beside them as a car came to a screeching stop. Both men turned to look as Colton Bale scrambled out of the driver's side door.

"Jude," he exclaimed, "are you okay?"

And seeing them both, together, reminded Jude of everything that had happened. The lies, the betrayal, how absolutely annihilated he had been, all of it surged through Jude like a relentless wave. That coupled with Eoin's obvious disinterest was overwhelming.

"Jude?" Colton said gently, walking around the front of his car, joining the two men on the sidewalk. "Are you all right?"

Jude took a deep breath, calmed, and centered, and then his dark eyes flicked to Colton's face. "It was a mistake to agree to have dinner, because a good working relationship is all I want with you. If I led you to believe it was anything else, I apologize." He turned his head to look at his ex. "We're done. You know we are. Have a good life, Tiernan."

The complete lack of passion in Jude's words told Tiernan that he was of no importance whatsoever. They were done; they would not even be friends, and Tiernan, who had never even entertained the possibility that he could not win Jude back, was dumbfounded. Normally he could correct his mistakes, but this one there was no fix for.

As Jude walked away, moving fast down the street, the two men stared after him, dumbfounded. He wanted neither of them, and the weight of what they had done finally sank in. The act of betrayal was irrevocable, and Jude was not the forgiving kind.

Jude focused on breathing. He cleared his head of everything but food. He had to prepare a meal fit for a guardian, dazzle Eoin with his culinary skills. If the man had made a courtesy trip to tell him that he had changed his mind about taking Jude as a mate, he would at least reward him for his integrity. It was the least Jude could do.

While walking home, he settled down, his heart no longer in his throat, able to find some semblance of his own self-respect and value. If Eoin no longer wanted him, someone would, someday. He was a good man. He had a good heart, and someone would want to keep him. Back in his apartment, Jude shed his trench coat and suit jacket along with his tie before unbuttoning his collar to get to work on dinner.

"Jude."

He looked across the room at Eoin Thral as he stood leaning in the door frame clad only in his deerskin breeches. Seeing the man, Jude knew that everything he'd thought about on his walk home was a lie. If Eoin no longer loved him, he had no idea what he would do. "I'm just gonna start dinner." Jude coughed, forcing as smile as he took out his silver cuff links and rolled up his sleeves. "I'll call you when it's ready. You just rest."

"Jude!" Eoin barked his name.

His eyes instantly returned to his mate.

"I thought I was dreaming," Eoin told the smaller man. "I had such before as being returned to your arms, only to wake and find I was still cold and wet and covered in the blood of other men."

Jude was back to not being able to breathe.

"You will forgive me now and know that all I wanted was to be in your bed with you wrapped tight about me." Eoin's jaw clenched, and his voice dropped to a husky whisper. "I love no other and want no other. You are my home."

Jude's heart hurt.

"You will come to me now, for I need you."

Jude moved slowly back across the room, stopping several feet from the big man.

"Come," Eoin motioned him closer.

"I don't want to hurt you."

"You cannot hurt me, love," Eoin said, giving his mate a wicked grin. "But I would you try."

Jude wanted to move but found that he was still frozen, rooted to the spot on the floor. The roller-coaster ride that his life had been since he met this man seemed to be coming to a stop, but just the last hour, like the last scary dip at the end, had left him shaken and unsure.

Eoin realized that playfulness alone would not soothe the man. The foundation of love and trust was just newly built when it had been asked to stand alone without support. What Eoin had to convey now was that he was there to stay, there to reinforce the love they shared and would not again abandon his mate. "I will never again be parted from you, Jude Shea," Eoin said, "as I cannot live without my heart… my _cairn_."

The words combined with the longing in the dark eyes were more than Jude could bear. He rushed forward, his faith in the man and his love restored, and Eoin saw clearly the absolute trembling joy of his mate. He flung himself into Eoin's waiting arms, and when he lifted his head, the guardian bent and kissed him.

Eoin took absolute possession of Jude's mouth, licking, sucking, the kiss hungry and devouring, all the need and want fueling it, the guardian wanting to reclaim what was rightfully his: the man in his arms.

Jude had to pull back to breathe. "I want to take care of you… please let me."

"I will have my mate now," Eoin growled at him, moving fast, grabbing Jude's wrist in a vise-like grip, crossing quickly to the couch and sitting down with Jude in his lap, "I am well enough. I need no physician to mend me. Only you."

Jude looked over the man's black eye, the red splotches on his jaw, his throat, the split lip, and the stitched wound on his left shoulder. He caught his breath. "You look terrible."

Eoin closed his eyes under his mate's roaming hands, loving the feel of the warm skin on his chilled flesh. "I care not." Eoin just wanted Jude closer; he ran his hands up the muscular thighs, scooting him forward so that Jude's groin was pressed to his abdomen.

"I need to feed you."

"I will claim what is mine first," Eoin told him, "so fetch me what you would use to ease me inside you, *cairn.*"

But Jude was fairly certain that Eoin was doing what he thought Jude wanted and not what the guardian needed. "First things first," Jude said, rising up off his mate's lap. "Lemme show you something, okay?"

Eoin growled again, but Jude's smile was too warm, too disarming to fight. The guardian realized that whatever Jude wanted, he would do. So much had happened since he had seen him last, so much blood had been spilled, so many lives lost, and only the promise of his mate had kept him sane. So he let Jude take his hand and lead him to the bathroom.

The warm water that fell effortlessly was a marvel to the guardian, as was the soapy gel, the loofah, and the amazing, removable shower head. Jude's hands all over him, the massaging fingers in his hair, sliding down his back, so gentle, so tender—it was a revelation. The concern the man took was beyond imagining, because no one had ever cared if Eoin was in pain. Only Jude, ever, had cared.

"When we're done here, I'm going to feed you, and then you need to rest." Jude smiled, his face turned up to Eoin, the big brown eyes holding his gaze. "We'll talk in the morning."

"No." Eoin's voice caught, cracking. "I need you."

And Jude understood and so stroked his hands slowly, tenderly over Eoin's bruised and battered body, sliding across the broad shoulders, over the massive chest, down the rippling abdomen and lower to the hard, aching shaft.

"I cannot… I missed—"

"Be still," Jude ordered his mate, sinking to his knees and taking Eoin into his hot, wet mouth.

There were so many words Eoin had saved up to say, but they were gone suddenly, all his rehearsed declarations forgotten, his mind blank but for Jude. The skillful tongue swirling over his cock, the laving and licking, the strong, exquisite suction—it was all too overwhelming for the guardian. His groan was loud, ragged, and full of complete and utter surrender.

"Jude," he yelled, "stop!"

But Jude had no intention of stopping, instead swallowing the entire long, thick length of the man down his throat. Eoin had to clutch the tiled wall of the shower to keep from falling to his knees as he watched Jude, that beloved mouth stretched around him, those beautiful lips sliding over his skin. Feeling the voracious sucking, he was done.

Jude heard the panting, felt the fingers sliding through his hair to hold him still, and lifted his own hands to Eoin's ass, urging him forward to fuck his mouth. It was more than Eoin could bear, more than his mind could take in and process. Every piece of him, every part, belonged to his mate, and with the power Jude held, he wanted only to give Eoin pleasure. He only wanted to love him and sate him. Eoin's balls drew up tight, a buzzing current of electricity starting at the base of his spine and rushing through him, setting fire to his heart, soul, and mind; all of it exploding out of him and into Jude's mouth.

Eoin stood frozen, his eyes riveted on his younger, smaller lover as Jude swallowed and sucked until he was limp and spent. Only when the last shudder tore through Eoin did Jude rise and stand in front of the guardian.

"Stay here."

Eoin did as he was told, stood still under the cascading warmth and let the water soothe his muscles and the heat sink into his skin. When Jude returned, turned off the water, and gestured him forward, all the guardian could do was obey.

"I want you to lie down with me," he told Eoin softly.

He wanted to grab Jude, throw him over his shoulder, and hurl him down on the bed. He wanted to, but every last drop of energy he possessed was gone. Eoin could do nothing but allow Jude to lead him from the shower, wrap him in towels, and walk him to the bedroom. Once he was seated on the bed, he realized that the sheets were new.

"I want everything to be as perfect as it can for you."

Eoin tried to tell his mate that the only perfect he needed was him, but he was so close to collapsing he didn't dare risk it. All Jude's small considerations were a wonder to him: going to gather food, the clean sheets, bathing him... Eoin was simply overwhelmed.

Jude led him to the bed and had Eoin stretch out before he covered him with the sheet and comforter. To be wrapped in a cocoon of warmth, to be safe and loved... what more could Eoin ask? When the petting began a deep sigh rose up out of him.

"Close your eyes," Jude ordered him softly, his fingers sliding through Eoin's long glossy black hair, down the back of his neck to between his shoulder blades. He rubbed gentle circles and told Eoin how much he had missed him.

There was no way to remain conscious. Eoin passed out instead of falling asleep, and Jude was very pleased with himself as he got up to go cook the guardian's meal. He was so happy that it was Friday night, because now he had two days to do nothing but talk to his mate and explain quaint customs like takeout food and coffee and indoor plumbing and television. Jude smiled, just thinking about he and Eoin watching movies together in bed. He couldn't wait.

EOIN woke in the middle of the night so tense and hard that he was sure he was growling. Sitting up in bed he realized he was alone. Where the hell was his mate?

"Jude?" he called out but no response came back to him.

Eoin took a deep breath, trying to scent his mate, and immediately a wave of need rolled through him. The pheromones were drowning him, and when he rose in one powerful, graceful movement, he realized that his body, even in so short a time, was healing. It confirmed exactly what he had believed from the second he saw the man: Jude was all he needed.

Padding out to the couch, Eoin stood silent and frozen, suddenly tense because Jude was not there. He smelled Jude, saw the still steaming cup of tea and the opened book, and heard soft music playing. Jude had been there moments before; he must have just missed him. But what would prod Jude to leave? He checked the fire escape and the bathroom, no Jude. He was alone and he hated it. Walking to the door he opened it, and immediately the scent of his mate hit him. Eoin stalked back to the bedroom to get his pants.

Jude was standing in the lobby of his building talking as fast as he could to try and get Tiernan Saunders out the front door. The two men who had come with him were standing at the inner door and outer security door respectively.

"Just let me come up." Tiernan was smiling at Jude, taking in the lean frame of his ex-lover, the V-line where his hip met his pelvis, the sweatpants barely on.

"Go home," Jude told him for the hundredth time. "You're drunk, Tiernan."

"Jude… baby." He leered drunkenly. "C'mere. Lemme take care of you."

Jude looked past him at two of Tiernan's friends who had never been his, Shane and Rick. Both men had indulged Tiernan's drunken notion to drive over to Jude's apartment and try and get in the man's bed. They thought it was funny when their drunken friend was plastered to Jude's door calling for him to let him the hell inside. Tiernan wanted Jude back in the worst way, and even more, he wanted to fuck him. That he had gone into graphic detail in the car had made both his friends horny as hell. If Tiernan wasn't given admittance, which both men were pretty sure he wouldn't be, based on how loud he was and the level of alcohol in his system, Rick Adams was going to see if Jude could be convinced to let him stay. Between the erotic memories Tiernan had confessed and looking at Jude now, Rick was more than ready to be the next guy in Jude Shea's bed… until his eyes lifted to the man who suddenly filled his vision.

Eoin Thral descended the stairs in nothing but his deerskin breeches. They were not belted but they were tight and so clung to his lean hips like a second skin. He was barefoot and shirtless, and Shane, who was at the outer door, had never seen a more beautiful man. The rippling muscles—bulging biceps and triceps—the way the pants molded to the muscular thighs and calves; he was mouth-watering. The black silky hair hit and spilled slightly past his shoulders, and the dark eyes were deep and liquid.

"Jesus. Who's that?" Shane barely got out.

Tiernan had taken a step back from Jude when he saw Eoin coming down the stairs behind him. Somehow he just knew that the huge man was looking for his ex.

Jude turned and saw Eoin, and his smile was instant and automatic. All the boiling anger Eoin felt evaporated in the face of the love on his mate's face. How could he feel a murderous, seething rage when the man looked at him like that?

"What are you about, *cairn*?" he growled at Jude, stopping beside him, his hand instantly sliding up the bare back to close over Jude's shoulder.

Jude trembled under the touch, and Eoin felt the ripple of heat flare through him. "I didn't want anyone to wake you up, and these guys were at my door, so I walked them back down here."

Eoin understood then. The man swaying in front of Jude was his old lover, and he had gotten drunk and come pounding on Jude's door looking to get in his bed. "He will away."

"Yes," Jude agreed, looking at Shane and Rick. "Come take him, you guys."

"Who the fuck is this?" Tiernan asked loudly. "Your new boyfriend? You're fucking Neanderthals now?"

Before Eoin could move, Jude stepped in front of Tiernan. "This is Eoin, and yeah... he's my boyfriend. He just moved in."

"That quick, huh, from when I saw you before to now, he moved in that fast? That's bullshit, Jude, and we both know it."

"'Tis not in the man to lie," Eoin said, reaching around his mate and grabbing a hold of Tiernan's sweater. The man was off his feet and dragged forward to the guardian. "And now you need to go and return not. The man is mine."

Tiernan would have argued, would have told him to go to hell, and would have said that Jude made his own choices, but from the way his ex was looking up at Eoin Thral, Tiernan saw clearly what was there. Jude was looking at the giant in a way he had never seen but recognized nonetheless. It was as clear as day that Jude was in love.

"C'mon," Jude said, hands closing on Eoin's forearm, trying to get him to release Tiernan. "I wanna talk to you upstairs."

"This man—"

"Means nothing," Jude assured him, "so let him go."

Eoin shoved Tiernan back hard, but the man found his footing and just stared.

"Goodbye," Jude dismissed his ex without another thought and took Eoin's hand to lead him up the stairs.

The guardian found that he enjoyed his mate's fingers laced with his, loved listening to Jude talk about how first thing in the morning they needed to go shopping for clothes, and liked the light that came into the smaller man's eyes when he started talking about shoes. It was adorable.

"You're not gonna be weird about me taking care of you financially for awhile are you?" Jude asked the big man as they reached the door to the apartment. "'Cause once you start selling your furniture you can pitch in money too."

Eoin locked the door behind his mate, putting the chain on after the deadbolt. "I will care for you, *cairn*, and you for me. As soon as I am able I will do the same as you, but I must find my way in your world as you had to find yours in mine."

A big, strong, strapping man without the macho bullshit? He was too good to be true. Jude moved forward but stopped himself.

"Why do you keep yourself from me?" Eoin scowled at him, having lifted his hands to catch Jude in his arms and letting them fall back to his sides.

"I need to be more careful." Jude winced. "You're hurt, and I could have—"

"No." Eoin cut him off, grabbing his bicep and yanking him forward into his arms. He was pleased that when Jude lifted his lips for the kiss, questing for Eoin's mouth, that he found it in a hard, bruising kiss that was more bite than anything else.

Jude's arms wrapped around Eoin's neck as he deepened the kiss, clutching him tighter, smiling against the man's mouth as he felt the shudder run through him. Eoin held Jude against his heart as he pulled back for breath only to lick and bite Jude's lips. It was like being mauled, and Jude loved it. The massive man was not a gentle lover; he was all about primal sexual power and surging, devouring heat. His lovemaking was raw, dominant, and bruising, and there was never a time that Jude came away without marks. He hoped it stayed that way forever.

Jude hit the bed before he realized he'd been dropped down onto it; he was more surprised to find that his sweats were gone and he was sprawled out naked before his lover. The wicked gleam in Eoin's eyes was enough to suck the breath from Jude's lungs.

"God, I missed you," Jude said, swallowing hard, amazed at how much he had changed in so short a time. Learning to trust again, loving harder and more than he ever had, relinquishing control that he never thought he would or could. At first glance, Eoin Thral did not seem to be the kind of man Jude needed, but it turned out that the big, scary guardian was perfect for him.

Eoin sank to his knees in front of Jude, hooked his legs up over his shoulders, cupped his mate's beautiful ass in his callused hands and then bent forward and sucked Jude's cock down his throat. Jude had enough time to yell the man's name before his back bowed as he arched up off the bed. He was devoured, and in moments he was panting for Eoin to stop what he was doing and pound him through the floor.

"Where?" Eoin gasped, releasing his mate's hard, swollen shaft. His own cock was wet and dripping inside his leather pants, his balls aching and tightening. Jude's uninhibited response was already bringing him so close.

Jude pointed at the nightstand, and Eoin rose and went to it. The bottle there was small, but the slick fluid inside was like nothing Eoin had ever felt in his life. Jude's eyes on him, hungry and glazed, as Eoin coated his shaft sent surging heat straight to Eoin's balls. When he slid his coated fingers into the man's ass, Jude's urgent pleading became a demand.

"Eoin... now!"

The guardian settled himself between Jude's thighs, lifted him, and pushed gently against his entrance. A low, ragged moan was all Eoin needed. Thrusting forward, he buried himself in his mate's hot, willing body in one long brutal plunge, and he felt, finally, like he was home. The muscles in Jude's ass hugged him so tight, squeezing and clenching as he stroked Jude's beautiful cock to the same rhythm he set as he pounded in and out of the puckering, flexing hole. Jude was folded in half, the backs of his thighs plastered to Eoin's chest as the man rammed his massive shaft deeper and deeper inside of him.

"Eoin!" Jude screamed his name as the orgasm roared through him, peaking at the same time that his lover's began, the muscles in Jude's ass all gripping at once, swallowing Eoin in a slick, heated, velvet vise. Just for a second the guardian thought he'd gone blind.

As Eoin remained buried in his mate, unable to move, riding out the aftershocks of his bone-numbing orgasm, he wondered what he would not do for the man under him. He loved Jude body and soul, and whatever he wanted, for the rest of Eoin's life, Eoin would do.

"You swear you don't have to go back," Jude pressed him.

Eoin could only nod. "I am yours, Jude Shea."

And with that Jude spread his legs, and Eoin fell forward very ungracefully and pinned his mate to the bed. Jude didn't mind that he couldn't breathe. What did he need air for? He had his man.

WHEN Eoin opened his eyes again he was alone. For a second he thought maybe it had all been a really hot, really long, really vivid dream about his mate before he heard Jude banging around in the kitchen.

"Jude?"

Jude walked into the bedroom a minute later, hair tousled, lips swollen from being kissed, and his eyes soft and unguarded. Eoin felt his chest tighten just looking at him. "Jude." He smiled, content to just look at his mate.

"Hey baby." Jude smiled lazily. "I heated everything up I made earlier so you can—"

"Come here to me."

Jude moved to the bed and leaned over to kiss Eoin.

The guardian tangled his fingers in the hair at the back of his head and kept him there, his lips parting for him as Eoin drew his tongue deep into his mouth. He rose up so he had leverage and eased Jude down under him, lying down between his legs.

"So you're not hungry," Jude chuckled into his mouth as Eoin slid his hands down over the hard, bumpy plains of his sculpted abdomen.

"Did I say I was not hungry, Jude Shea?"

"God," Jude moaned loudly.

Eoin yanked down the sweatpants and found only bare skin. Under his stroking touch Jude's eyes drifted closed, and he called Eoin's name like a chant. When his hand closed around Jude, he called louder, urgently.

"Yes, *cairn*." He smiled, his voice raw and throaty.

"Eoin," Jude breathed, his lips still brushing over his mate's, no contact broken.

"I will try to be gentle," Eoin promised, licking Jude's lush lips.

"Eoin." His breath came in pants as he barely stifled a moan.

"Is that a yes, love?"

"Yes… yes… please!"

Eoin wanted to kiss him some more. The sound from deep inside, it rose up out of him, surfacing like all Jude's feelings did. He loved Eoin, needed him, this then the reason for his begging… the guardian was necessary.

EOIN had never eaten such a meal as the one Jude prepared for him. It was beyond anything he could have ever imagined. And the revelation that his mate could make such delights for him was too astonishing to put into words. His mate was both wanton and a good cook. Surely no man had ever been so blessed. The food put down in front of him and the way it all smelled drove every thought but his mate away. Watching Jude smile at him, listening to him talk about work, letting Eoin just eat—the guardian was afraid he was dreaming again.

"You will cook for me every night, then, *cairn*?"

"No," Jude said with a chuckle, "but I promise to eat *with* you every night. Sometimes we're gonna hafta go out."

Eoin had no idea what that meant, but as long as Jude took his evening meal with him, he was content. Just seeing how pleased the man was over Eoin praising his efforts was gratifying. It meant so much to Jude that Eoin appreciated him, and for that the guardian was thankful. He wanted to matter to Jude; in fact, he wanted to be the most important thing in Jude's life.

"How 'bout some more wine?"

Eoin shook his head. "I will have my mate now," he said, stopping Jude from what he was doing, making him put the plates down, leave the wine glasses alone, stop moving at all. "Come sit here." He smiled wickedly, patting his lap.

Instead, Jude sat down and turned to look at his lover.

"*Cairn*?"

"Tell me everything."

Eoin sighed deeply. "I am tired, *cairn*, I would—"

"Just like I figured." Jude nodded, standing up. "You need to sleep. Lemme help you back to bed."

Jude's care was nurturing, gentle, and loving, and Eoin realized he wanted none of that. There was time for succor and comfort later; now he needed heat and lust and to be buried to the hilt in his mate.

"You're shivering," Jude remarked worriedly, tucking in the comforter that he had wrapped Eoin in when they left the bedroom. "C'mon, let's get you back to bed."

Eoin gripped Jude's wrist tight before yanking him down into his lap.

"What's—"

"Drist is dead." Eoin cleared his throat as his hands settled on his mate's hips.

Jude's hands were immediately on the sides of Eoin's neck. "Oh honey, I'm so sorry."

The sympathy almost undid the guardian.

"What happened?"

Eoin could not be expected to recount all the horror stories. He could not explain how it felt to watch Drist, his fenris, his own leader, be killed by the king's man Cuyler Adon. Even taking the life of the man in return had not granted Eoin any solace.

How was he to convey to his mate the depth of the need in his baroness when she had begged Eoin to stay and become her fenris? Drelindah knew she was being selfish in her request of her guardian, asking him to turn his back on his mate, but she had been unable to stop herself.

She trusted Eoin the most after her beloved Drist, and with the older man gone, she was loathe to lose Eoin as well. But the request had become moot when the royal castle at Goren in the kingdom of Midrin was finally taken and Crispin Ebudai, laird of the outlanders, the rebels, was proclaimed lord protector of the realm and the Baroness of Saraso, his intended, Drelindah Holt, became his lady.

Crispin would serve faithfully the newly crowned archlord of Midrin, Bishop Rista Dumal. It turned out that Lyan Han, prefect of the deposed king, had been wrong when he had spoken those many months ago to Crispin; there were no barons at all who supported the king and his tyranny. Once the castle was stormed and prisoners taken, everyone swore fealty to the new archlord.

Eoin had been saddened, even after how bloody the siege had been, that the king was publically executed for his crimes. He was pleased that the queen and her infant son were spared. They were exiled and sent far across the sea; he hoped the prince would remain in obscurity forever and never learn of his birthright.

Eoin had accompanied Arius Sepo, Drelindah's newly appointed fenris, back to Saraso. The baroness, now the lord protector's lady, would remain at court with her husband, Crispin Ebudai, there to build a new state with the archlord. Drelindah's domo, Greshan Kai, was to take her place on the barony, and he, too, asked Eoin to remain with them. But the guardian had found his mate, his *cairn*, and it was time, finally time, for him to join Jude. He had no doubt that from the other guardians left alive, Orim, Vardeen, and Lazoore, that the barony would be in safe hands. Eoin, who had once dreamed of taking his mentor's place, begrudged Arius nothing. His only desire was to return to Jude. The life of a guardian was no longer Eoin's.

When Eoin walked from the holding in the middle of the night—with Greshan's reluctant blessing—he had left with nothing but the clothes on his back. He wanted only his freedom, and that had been granted him. There would be no more blood and gore, no more pain, and no more wondering if this would be the day he died. He wanted nothing more than to go to his home, to go where his mate was, and now he was there. All the concerns of Midrin were no longer his.

"Eoin?"

He reached out and cupped Jude's face in his hands. "Please, I will speak for days if it pleases you, but now... now you lay with me. There is no more I would do."

Why would Jude argue?

HOURS passed, and Eoin was aware only of an almost overwhelming feeling of happiness. As he lay draped across the small of Jude's back, he lifted his head to kiss above his tailbone, sucking at the same time. He had worn out the smaller man, and he smiled over that knowledge as he felt the steady rise and fall of his breathing.

"Are you sure you love me, then, *cairn*?" Eoin mumbled, rubbing his stubbled cheek over Jude's delicious skin, putting goose bumps all over the man.

"Yes," came the deep groan from Jude. "You know I do."

"I have asked much of you."

"Eoin." Jude shivered. "You're killing me. Try listening for once in your life."

He chuckled and moved lower to gently nuzzle Jude's ass, to bite softly before he slid his tongue over the same spot, licking him slowly and seductively.

"Oh God." The trembling response sounded almost pained.

"You missed me?" Eoin asked, since he had to hear Jude say it a hundred different times in a hundred different ways.

"Yes, baby," Jude barely got out. Eoin's tongue was distracting. "You know I did."

"I came as soon as I was able," Eoin said solemnly, his voice hoarse.

"I know," Jude assured him, shifting, needing to get up and out of the sticky, sweaty mess of the bed. He needed water. "Lemme up. I gotta show you another marvel of my world."

When he returned minutes later with ice cold water from the refrigerator, Eoin was astounded. It would take time for him to get used to such luxuries. When he noticed Jude staring down at him he smiled back.

"Tell me what so pleases you, _cairn_?"

"You in my bed," Jude said flatly.

Eoin's heart stopped. "Only you look at me as though I am beautiful."

"But you are beautiful… and hot and sexy as hell."

A shiver tore through the guardian. "Come here," he said as he made his voice soft and enticing. Jude moved quickly, getting back in bed, rising over Eoin, and straddling his hips.

"There's something else I—stop," Jude ordered him weakly as Eoin ran his hands up his thighs, his fingers massaging Jude's hot skin.

"I have to touch you. I missed you."

Jude just stared down at Eoin.

"Look at you," Eoin whispered.

The pale light from the street was illuminating half of Jude; the rest of him was in shadow. He looked like some conflicted angel, dark and light, all chiseled perfection and ethereal beauty. Jude smiled in the darkness, and the way he was looking at Eoin made the man's mouth go dry.

"Eoin," Jude murmured. His fingers were so gentle as they slid over his cheeks, his jaw, and down the length of his throat, stroking and caressing his burning skin.

Eoin pulled him closer, into his lap, his other hand under the pillow where he had tucked the bottle of lube they had been using. No one wanted to roll over on it and find it wedged into the middle of their back. Jude smiled when he heard the top open.

"Are you kidding?"

Eoin was not.

"What's with you?"

"I crave you, my mate," Eoin confessed, moving under Jude, pulling him forward so Jude's ass rested against Eoin's groin. "You feel good."

"We need to stop; we need sleep," Jude said, but there was no conviction in his voice, only a catch as Eoin's hands traveled up the backs of his lean muscular thighs.

"You need to take me back inside of you."

Jude's eyes were glazed as he looked down at Eoin before he leaned slowly back, stretching and arching, his arms braced behind him, hands on the guardian's legs as he held still above him.

Eoin ran his hands over him, one hand cupping Jude's ass and kneading the skin, bringing him forward, the angle just right, the lubed fingers of his other hand sliding inside of him and causing a deep shiver of pleasure.

"Your body begs for me."

Only a nod—it was all Jude could manage as Eoin wrapped a hand around his cock and stroked him slowly and deliberately. He watched Jude tremble before he lifted him and then lowered him, impaling him on the long, hard length of his shaft, filling his tight channel.

They moved together in their now-familiar rhythm, and Eoin's eyes never left Jude's until he closed them. And when he did, Eoin let his gaze slide all over his mate, the line of him, the smooth, flawless skin, the lean muscles, his stomach that was a carved work of art, and the way it rose and fell. Eoin heard his labored breathing, watched as he arched his back, completely surrendering to the demands of his body. The guardian loved it when Jude cried out his name.

JUDE was lying beside the man he loved, watching the guardian breathe, content to do nothing else as he reached out and traced one of the jet black eyebrows with his fingertip, then down the bridge of Eoin's nose to his lips.

"Is your plan to watch me sleep, then, *cairn*?" Eoin asked softly, smiling lazily.

"I might." Jude stared at him.

"Your lips are swollen, and there are bite marks on you...." Eoin took a breath, his voice bottoming out. "Your eyes are only just open... you look ravaged."

Jude nodded. "Well, you look the same."

"Good."

After several minutes of silence Jude spoke again. "I wanna talk to you."

"About what?"

"Everything."

Eoin grunted, that sounded daunting.

"Are you listening to me?"

"Yes," he lied, rolling over so he was looking down into Jude's bottomless brown eyes. "I will do as you say, *cairn*... anything you ask, I will do."

"You're not listening to me."

Eoin shifted closer to his mate, burying his fingers in the thick hair. "I am, *cairn*."

Jude swallowed hard, the feelings overwhelming for a moment, threatening to drown him. Eoin was there, safe and whole beside him; it was more than he had ever dreamed. "I just... I have so many questions," he said, his breath quivering, the whine in it full of need.

Eoin chuckled into his hair, leaning close, breathing him in. "There will be time, *cairn*; I will be here when your eyes open on the rise."

"In the morning, you mean."

"Aye, love, in the morning."

God, Jude loved him and couldn't get enough of him. "I missed just lying in bed with you."

"As did I," Eoin assured him, and he leaned over and kissed Jude so he'd know. He made sure he got all of Jude's mouth, kissing him thoroughly, deeply, letting him feel the jolt of need that ran through him. It was a demanding, consuming, and lingering kiss, Eoin's lips pressed to Jude's and making it last until he pulled away so he could breathe.

"God... the way you kiss me," Jude said. Eoin felt his breath on his face as his lips were still hovering over Jude's. "Don't stop."

Eoin slanted his mouth down over Jude's, kissing him so hard that the moaning was guttural, up from his soul.

"Eoin," he rasped out, gulping for air when he shoved the guardian off. "I could die from this."

"Come here," Eoin said gently, leaning back down.

"Wait." Jude pushed him back again. "I wanna talk to you."

"You are a tease, *cairn*." Eoin chuckled. "But I will have you."

"Are you listening to me?"

"No, Jude," Eoin sighed, staring down into his eyes. The guardian just wanted to bask in his mate's attention.

He scowled at Eoin, his hands sliding into his hair as his eyes closed under his touch. "I feel like I haven't seen you in years."

"Did you lose hope, then, of my return?"

"No, it was just hard."

"As it was for me, as well," Eoin said, leaning in close to kiss Jude's irresistible collarbone and then the side of his throat. "But well you know... you are my home, *cairn*. I will never stay away from my home."

Jude nodded because speech was beyond him.

"You know this." It was a statement.

Jude stared up at him, at his beautiful mouth, the way it curved, the dip under his nose now covered in many days of stubble. When he lifted his arms, inviting Eoin closer, the guardian leaned down and wrapped his mate in his arms. He hugged Jude tight as he rolled to his side, tucking his head under his chin, pressing him to his heart.

"You are my love," Eoin told the man in his arms.

"And you're mine," Jude said, his voice failing him at the end.

Eoin clutched his mate tighter, and again, for the thousandth time since he met the man, let the miracle of finding him flood him with absolute peace. It was a very great thing to find your way home.

Chapter Twelve

JUDE was so enjoying watching his mother and his partner that he didn't immediately realize that he himself was under scrutiny. When he finally felt the weight of the eyes on him, he turned slowly to face the firing squad.

"What?"

His brother's wife glared at him. "Are you kidding?"

He smiled at Megan Shea, only to have her lift her hand for him to talk to it. "Dad," he said with a chuckle, looking over at his father.

"It's not fair, Jude," he grumbled at his son. "I've been waiting for over twenty years to get in that kitchen, and he just saunters in here and gets invited after a day?"

They were all being ridiculous.

"I think you should take him back to where you found him," his brother Ben said pointedly, widening his eyes, glancing at his wife so Jude would understand the full severity of his crime.

"That would be tough," Jude addressed his brother.

"Not really." Ben smiled knowingly. "Just a quick trip through some fog, right?"

"Quit." Jude laughed at his brother, tickled by all of them, his irritated family, as the sliding glass door that led from the patio to the living room opened and three couples, one older, two younger, slipped into the room.

Jude's father, James Shea, rose to greet friends, Edward and Yvonne and their children, on behalf of himself and his wife, Barbara. It was going to be a full house for Christmas dinner, and the house already smelled amazing. When Yvonne froze suddenly, her husband was alarmed.

"What's wrong, honey?"

"Who's that?" Yvonne Hughes asked, pointing over at Eoin.

"Holy crap." Ed snorted out a laugh, looking at James. "There's someone in the kitchen with your wife while she's cooking. Does he know he's taking his life in his hands?"

"Not once in the twenty-two years that I've known her has that woman let me in the kitchen with her when she's cooking," Yvonne protested. "It's her *safe* place."

"She used her teacher voice to get me out last Easter," Ben told everyone.

"She just gives me this really indulgent smile until I leave," Megan grumbled.

"Oh, I get that too," Jude's father chimed in. "The patronizing smirk."

"Yeah, it's great, isn't it?" Megan scrunched up her face, her tone dripping with sarcasm.

"She threw an avocado at me the last time I tried to help her," Ed said as he continued to chuckle. "For heaven's sake, who is that?"

"Jude's new boyfriend," James Shea grunted, arching one eyebrow as he looked at his son. "I hate him. We all hate him."

The laughter bubbled up out of Jude. "Y'all are just jealous."

And it was true; they *were* jealous. Everyone wanted to spend time with Barbara Shea. She made you feel good just being around her, and because she so loved to cook, everyone wanted to spend that time with her, have her teach them, be able to just casually chat with her while she created masterpieces. But it was her time to be completely alone; the cooking gave her peace and needed solitude. She allowed no one near her until she called… until now.

Jude had seen his man wander into the kitchen with his mother and nearly choked when she lifted a spoon for Eoin to try the water chestnut and shallot dressing she made from scratch. For whatever reason, she saw the need in the man to be mothered and nurtured, and she was ready to step in and fill the vacant place in his life. She was ready to adopt him.

"Jude," Yvonne and Ed's oldest son Mark asked as he smiled over at him. "Is your boyfriend magic?"

What was the real answer to that?

At dinner as Eoin explained about his business, Jude was careful not to growl. Stopping by Eoin's studio/showroom in Oak Park always made Jude cranky. And it wasn't for any other reason than the people who were always there. Eoin Thral was hot, and not just to Jude. From interior decorators to designers to housewives, everybody was crazy about the man and his rustic furniture that was handmade to last a lifetime.

After his brother Ben created Eoin's identity for him a year ago, it had been Jude's turn to make the man into a household name. True to his word, Jude had launched a brilliant marketing campaign with a fully interactive web site that was glitch-free from day one. The business took off so fast that Eoin was forced to hire two other craftsmen, both older and meaner than he was. He had three salespeople who worked in the showroom and a very efficient woman from one of the top accounting firms in the city who came once a week to take care of the finances. Jude had made sure there would be no stray dog Eoin hired off the street taking care of his books. He wanted Eoin to be successful, and no one was going to sideline him.

The problem quickly became that the man was doing *too* well. People were *too* crazy about him, and he made himself far *too* accessible. Take, for instance, the very handsome man who had been talking to the ex-guardian when Jude arrived three nights ago to collect Eoin for the trip to the airport. The stranger had his hand on Eoin's shoulder as he stared into his eyes. It was revolting, and the way laughter followed every word Eoin uttered was revolting. Jude stood for a minute of it before he walked over and interrupted, reminding Eoin that they had a plane to catch. The mischievous smile he got in return let Jude know that he was not fooling his mate with his brisk manner and clipped words. Eoin knew jealousy when he heard it.

"Jude?"

Looking up he saw his mother smiling at him. "Sorry," he said, realizing he'd been growling. It was a terrible habit.

After dinner, Jude was in the kitchen, as always the one to start the dishes while everyone else was still having dessert and coffee. When Eoin found him, Jude had the radio cranked up and was dancing beside the sink as he sang along with the music. Eoin leaned against the door frame instead of walking in; content to simply watch the man he loved. After a few minutes, however, he realized that his body was responding to seeing Jude's move. The sensual sway of hips, the leaned-back head, the parted lips, it all reminded Eoin of other more primal rhythms. Dishes needed to be finished so he could take his mate to bed.

As everyone shuttled plates into the kitchen, it was the women that noticed how thick the air was getting in the room. Everyone agreed that Jude and his new boyfriend made a nice pair, the tall, buff furniture-maker and his smaller, leaner partner. Eoin with his dark tanned skin, black hair, and eyes and Jude's olive complexion, huge brown eyes, and tousled curls. The idea of them in bed was hot, and when Megan mentioned it to her mother-in-law, Barbara Shea gasped in pretend horror before batting her away. Inwardly she could not have been happier that her son had finally found someone worthy of him, worthy of his heart, worthy to care for it. She had known the moment she saw the way Eoin Thral looked at her son that he was a keeper. And he needed her, too, needed to be mothered; it was better than she could have ever dreamed. It was as though Eoin and Jude were made for each other.

Eoin decided that having a family was both a blessing and a curse. Being accepted and included was amazing, but trying to follow his mate upstairs to where he had retreated proved impossible. After another two hours spent rolling dice and drawing pictures, Jude's mother finally took pity on the man and told him to go on up to bed. The way he bolted from the room made everyone laugh.

"They're getting married next month in Vermont." Barbara sighed, looking back at the assembled people in her living room. "Isn't it wonderful?"

Everyone agreed that it was.

Eoin arrived in the bedroom to find Jude asleep with an open book on his chest, cozy under a thick, down comforter. He stood for a moment staring at his mate before he walked in and locked the door behind him. Eoin didn't think he would ever get used to the simple joy of crawling into a warm bed on a cold snowy night and curling up next to the man he loved. He was pleased that Jude's parents had insisted on everyone making the trip to Lake Tahoe for the holidays, because it was nice that it was frigid and icy outside and safe and warm inside. It would be hard to leave in two more days.

Moving the book to the nightstand, Eoin lay down and rolled Jude over into his arms, turning off the light, only the flames from the fireplace now illuminating the room. Jude was in his pajamas, and there was something about them that Eoin found extremely arousing. Although there was not much that Eoin did not find sexy about Jude Shea, especially the way he molded his body to Eoin's, even in sleep. The flannel-covered leg that slid between his, grazing his penis in the process, made Eoin groan with need. But Jude was tired; so Eoin would not flip him over on his back, lift his legs over his shoulders, and plunge down into him. It was too late; he just needed to go to sleep. But even as Eoin contemplated getting up and changing out of his jeans and dress shirt, he knew he wouldn't be able to close his eyes. Jude was tormenting him, and the man had no idea.

Soft lips pressed against the base of Eoin's throat, but he was sure the contact was incidental. A hand slid down his abdomen, but Eoin tensed and didn't react even when Jude's head lolled sideways and his warm, wet breath slid over his left nipple, hardening the nub to granite. He prayed for strength. The sound that rose up out of the man, almost a purr, made Eoin grit his teeth. When Jude finally pressed his hardened, lengthened shaft into Eoin's hip, rubbing, needing friction to ease the ache, Eoin slipped his hand under the drawstring pajama bottoms and wrapped his fingers around him.

"Oh," Jude moaned, his back bowing as he began slowly slipping his cock in and out of Eoin's callused fist.

He was only half awake, and Eoin loved that, loved that even unconscious, Jude's body craved his, craved his touch. As he continued to stroke his lover's velvety hardness, he could feel Jude's heart beating in his swollen shaft.

"Turn over," Eoin suggested in Jude's ear, and he smiled evilly as the request was obeyed, Jude whimpering in his sleep as his desire grew.

He threw back the covers, pulled off all their clothes, grabbed the lube from where he had stashed it under his pillow, and settled himself slowly, carefully, between Jude's thighs. He warmed the lube between his palms before coating his own throbbing shaft. Eoin knew he was already leaking pre-come; he smelled it even before he saw the pearly beads on the flared head of his own penis.

Eoin took in the long, sensual line of his mate's back, the slope down and then up to the swell of the firm, round buttocks. Unable to resist a moment more, he eased one slick finger between Jude's ass cheeks and stroked inside. The instant trembling accompanied by a deep, guttural groan told him that his ministrations were wanted, appreciated, and needed. He felt the tight ring of clenching muscle loosen almost instantly, ready to receive the second finger that immediately joined the first.

Watching Jude's tight little ass swallow his fingers, having quickly added a third, feeling the pressure exerted, seeing Jude reach under himself and stroke his own cock was more than Eoin could bear. When he withdrew his fingers, Jude whimpered and whined, sleep falling slowly away as his face was shoved down into the mattress, his hips grabbed roughly, his ass hoisted up.

"Beg me," Eoin growled at his mate, wanting as always to hear both permission and surrender.

Jude turned his face to the side, his body hot and pulsing with need. "Please...." He sucked in a breath. "Oh please...."

Eoin spread Jude's ass cheeks, saw the fluttering pink hole, and pressed gently at the entrance, prepared to plunge deep into his mate with one brutal stroke. At the last moment, he changed his mind and instead sank slowly into the opening one heartbeat at a time, feeling every second of the undulating slide into the hot, tight channel. He was sure the pace was going to kill him. The sensations were too much, too overpowering, and when Eoin was buried to the hilt in his mate's ass, he found himself at the mercy of desire that rose off Jude like steam.

"Why are you waiting?" Jude's voice was strangled, quivering with frustration as he turned his head and looked over his shoulder at his lover. "I need you... I need... Eoin, please."

The "please" could not be denied. The thrust forward, hard and deep, made Jude cry out his lover's name as his prostate was grazed in the process and on each subsequent stroke.

"The words, *cairn*," Eoin demanded in Jude's ear, "give me the words."

"I love you," Jude's moan was ragged. His brain shutting down, overwhelmed with sensations: his stretched and full hole, the hand jerking him off in a strong, slippery grip, the lips on his shoulder before the teeth. "Please... harder... Eoin...."

The begging was like a siren's song, irresistible. Eoin tightened his hold on the narrow hips in his hands and drove down into his lover, impaling Jude on the hot, hard length of enormous cock only to pull out and ram himself back in, the motion repeated with ever-quickening strokes, each one more hammering and pounding and more brutal than the last.

Jude's back bowed; his head was thrown back as he lost himself in his splintering orgasm, chanting his lover's name like a litany. The muscles clamping down on Eoin's shaft, Jude's orgasm was amazing to feel, see, and hear. Eoin filled his mate's tight channel as he found his own release seconds later. And he meant to move, had thought to pull out of his mate's shuddering body, but when Jude collapsed down onto the bed, Eoin's cock was still held within the clenching muscles in his mate's ass. Leaving the quivering hole as aftershocks pulsed through it was not something Eoin could manage. He ended up crushing Jude under him.

"Air," Jude chuckled huskily, gasping for breath, winded by the solid chest at his back.

Eoin eased gently from his mate and laid down his back beside him. "I squashed you again, love… I am sorry."

The man wasn't sorry one bit, and Jude knew it and loved it.

"It's okay." Jude exhaled, his eyes drifting closed, a smile curving his lips. "You can squash me any time you like."

Eoin reached for Jude, gathering him in his arms and holding him tight. It felt so good to hold his mate to his heart, to feel the warm breath on his throat and the bare skin plastered to his. Sometimes in the morning he had to peel Jude off him because sweat and semen had glued them together during the night. And even though Jude grumbled about having to be stripped from his lover, Eoin knew he wouldn't change it. It was good to know, to be certain that all his feelings were returned, never having even a doubt that he was loved.

Just the way Jude looked at him, touched him in passing, or kissed him for no reason sent waves of happiness through the big man. Jude's anger gave him a similar reaction, as he explained that he was not Eoin's maid and loading the washing machine was in fact not too hard for the ex-guardian to grasp. Every time Jude argued with him, yelled at him, or got annoyed with him, Eoin felt a rush of exhilaration because Jude cared enough to rant at him, thus proving that he was loved. And Jude could not stay mad at a man looking at him with such soft loving eyes, so the flashes of heat dissipated quickly, more often than not dissolving into slow, sensual make-up sex. Eoin was a strong proponent of resolving conflicts in bed. He told Jude this often.

"I'm not sorry I woke you," Eoin grunted smugly, nuzzling his face into Jude's silky curls, "and you didn't seem to mind."

"No, you can wake me up anytime." Jude smiled, closing his eyes, loving the feel of Eoin's hand lazily and possessively sliding up and down his back, as though the man were savoring the feel of his skin. It sent a shiver down his spine.

Eoin interpreted the trembling as cold and so reached for the comforter, throwing it over both him and his mate, snuggling them together in a cocoon of warmth.

"I'm not cold," Jude clarified sleepily, breathing in Eoin's musky scent, "I'm just happy. I have everything now, and it's all because of you. I could die happy right—"

"You will not die." Eoin clutched the man tighter in his arms. Sometimes when Jude walked away from him in the morning, leaving to walk to the train platform, sometimes… just for a second… Eoin couldn't breathe. There was a flush of anxiety, an instant of terror that tragedy would befall the man, and Eoin's life would come to a screeching halt. It happened less and less as time went by but still… every now and then… Eoin would want to run after his mate and drag him back home to the safety of their small two-story house in Oak Park.

Eoin loved his house, loved all the windows, and the fireplace, and the way the kitchen overlooked the back yard, and knowing when he opened the door at the end of the day that Jude would be there. The idea that Jude would ever not be there terrified the big man.

"What are you thinking about?" Jude asked, drawing Eoin's attention back to him. "'Cause you're a million miles away."

"You will be with me always," Eoin said firmly, clutching Jude even tighter, pressing him to his chest.

"Yes, I will," Jude assured him, knowing that Eoin's desire to protect and shelter him would never change. The big man had the heart of a warrior, of a guardian, and he could not change his nature anymore than Jude could change his. Not that Jude would ever ask. He loved the way Eoin Thral loved him, counted on it, demanded it, and needed it. The man belonged to him and so did his fierce heart.

"Sleep now, *cairn*." Eoin yawned, at peace again. "As we must rise early to go with your mother to a sale."

Jude snorted out a laugh. "Pardon me?"

"I'm not sure what she...." Eoin huffed out a breath, giving Jude a final squeeze before rolling over on his back, rubbing his eyes. "What is an after Thanksgiving Day sale?"

Jude turned his head so Eoin wouldn't see him smile.

"She spoke of Black Friday."

Eoin made it sound ominous and Jude bit his lip to keep silent.

"She said we had to be up before dawn to reach the mall. Was she in earnest?"

Jude could not control the laughter that came up out of him. The others were so jealous of Eoin being his mother's favorite, but clearly there were drawbacks. Like waking up to go shopping with her at four-thirty in the morning—only her favorite got invited along to do that.

"You will go with me, of course," Eoin said matter-of-factly, not a doubt in his mind.

Another snort of laughter as Jude rolled over on his side and closed his eyes. "Not even if you paid me."

"Jude Shea!" Eoin was appalled. "You will keep to your warm bed while I rise to go out into the cold without even a farewell or a meal?"

"She'll stop for coffee on the way, and if you're lucky, she'll get you a doughnut." Jude chuckled, feeling Eoin spoon around him, the hard chest at his back, the muscular thighs against his ass.

"I want you with me," Eoin said, kissing a line up the side of Jude's neck.

Jude cackled softly. "Nope, that's all you, buddy."

The low growl followed by a playful nibble made Jude smile. "There are other ways to convince you, *cairn*."

Jude knew then that the persuasion was about to take a very hot, very carnal turn. He knew, too, that more than likely he would end up bleary-eyed, sleep-deprived, and barely awake in the backseat of his mother's Toyota Corolla the following morning.

"You will say yes to me," Eoin told him, kissing a wet line down his mate's spine.

"Yes," Jude sighed out his agreement. It was true; he would do anything for Eoin Thral, even brave the mall the day after Thanksgiving. And that would be truly terrifying even for a guardian.

MARY CALMES currently lives in Honolulu, Hawaii, with her husband and two children and hopes to eventually move off the rock to a place where her children can experience fall and even winter. She graduated from the University of the Pacific (ironic) in Stockton, California, with a bachelor's degree in English literature. Due to the fact that it is English lit and not English grammar, do not ask her to point out a clause for you, as it will so not happen. She loves writing, becoming immersed in the process, and falling into the work. She can even tell you what her characters smell like. She works at a copy store but has been unable to incorporate that into a book… yet. She also buys way too many books on Amazon.

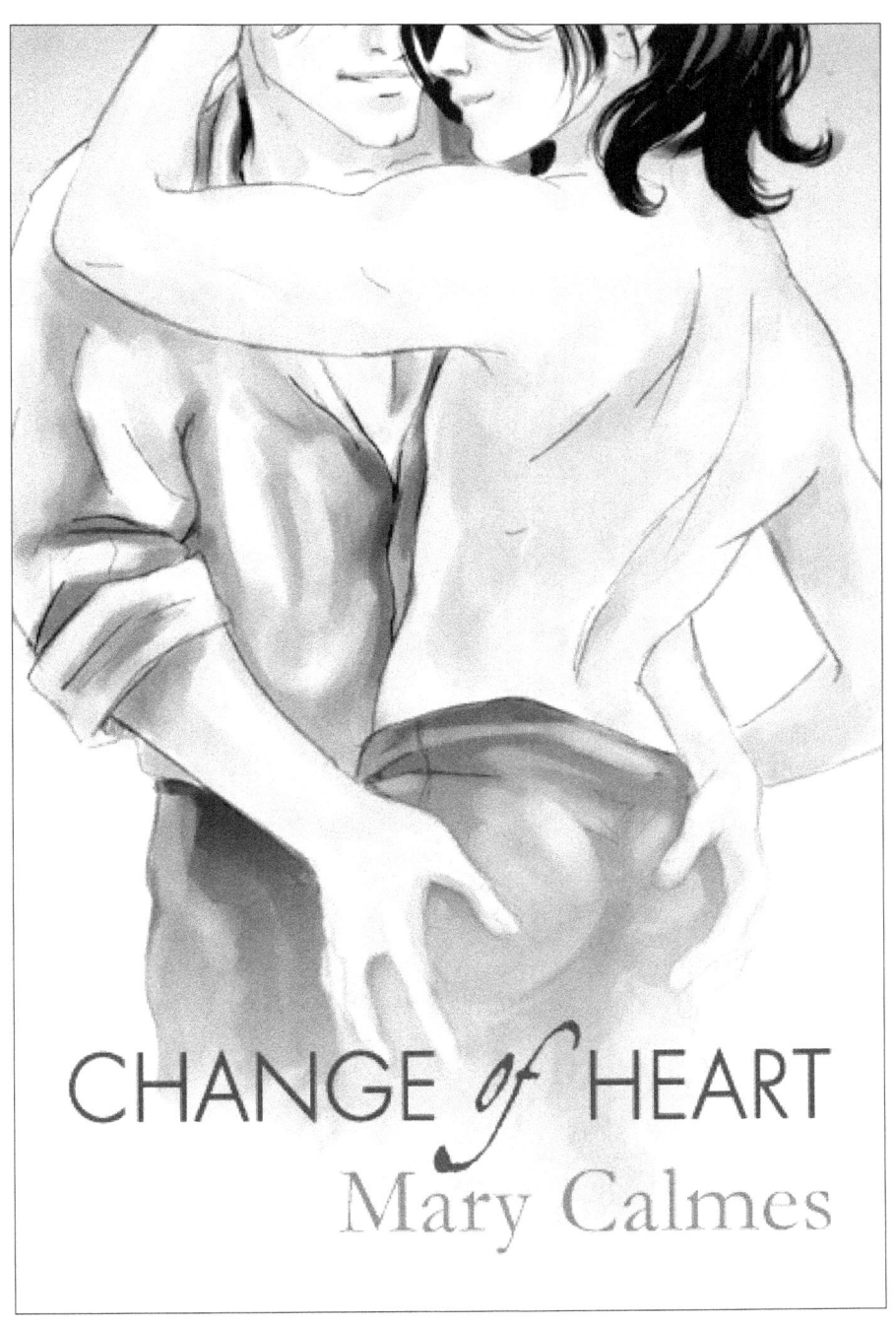

CHANGE *of* HEART
Mary Calmes

http://www.dreamspinnerpress.com

Other Paranormal Romance
from DREAMSPINNER PRESS

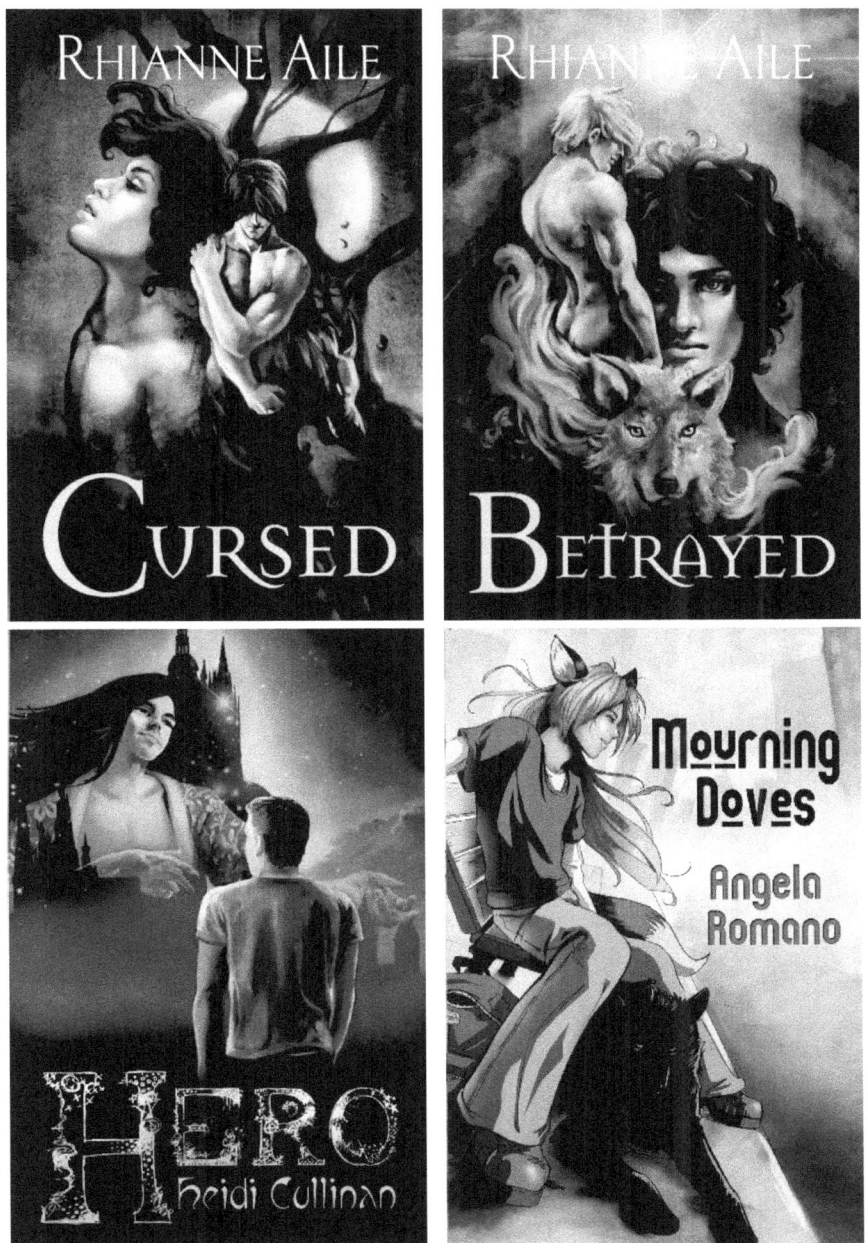

www.ingramcontent.com/pod-product-compliance
Lightning Source LLC
Chambersburg PA
CBHW071356250626
47159CB00004B/1634